ORC'S FATE

MONSTER MATE HUNT, BOOK 2

AVA ROSS

ENCHANTED STAR PRESS

ORC'S FATE

Monster Mate Hunt Book 2

Lumen Clan

Copyright © 2023 Ava Ross

All rights reserved.

Cover Art: Moonshot Covers

Editing: JA Wren and Owl Eyes Proofs & Edits

SERIES BY AVA

Mail-Order Brides of Crakair

Brides of Driegon

Fated Mates of the Ferlaern Warriors

Fated Mates of the Xilan Warriors

Holiday with a Cu'zod Warrior

Galaxy Games

Alien Warrior Abandoned

Beastly Alien Boss

Bride of the Fae

A Sci-Fi Holiday Tail

Monsterville, USA

Monster on Board

(co-written with Alana Khan)

Love at First Orc

Monster Mate Hunt

Single Titles

Dad Bod Dragon

Mated to the Dragon

Jasmine's Enchanted Genie

Swamp Thing (You Make My Heart Sing)

You can find her books on Amazon.

ORC'S FATE

Can a lonely widow and an orc with secrets find true love together?

Lyneth

After my husband's death, my village pushes me into the forest during the monster mate hunt, where I'll be claimed as an orc's bride.

I've vowed I'll never love another, but then I'm claimed by Madr, a strong, handsome orc who I suspect is hiding secrets. On his dragon-like vox, he flies with me toward his home. His warm arms keep me safe, and his teasing touch makes me reconsider every assumption I made about my past and my future. Do I dare give my heart to an orc?

Madr

When I abdicated the orc throne, I planned to live a simple life. I never expected the fates to bind me to Lyneth or that I'd fall for her so fast. But someone's out to kill me, and if I don't stop them, I won't survive long enough to claim my new bride.

Orc's Fate is Book 2 in the Monster Mate Hunt Series. Expect a seductive orc prince with a creative. . . (cough), size difference, her awakening, only one bed/forced proximity, a mourning woman finding new love, fated mates, plus a fantasy world you'll want to live in. HEA guaranteed. Each book is standalone, but the series is more fun if read in order.

Books in Order:
Orc's Mate
(a prequel novel)
Orc's Craving
Orc's Fate
Orc's Maiden
Orc's Captive
Orc's Taming

CHAPTER I
LYNETH

Tonight, I would have to give my body and soul to a fearsome orc.

Each year for the past eleven, my village sent two women into the forest to be claimed by orcs in exchange for protection from horrifying creatures called the shaydes.

The shaydes would kill us. As for the orcs?

They wanted to *mate* with us.

"It's time," Guardsman Kael said sadly. He laid his hand on my shoulder, squeezing gently. "Say the word, and I'll do all I can to keep this atrocity from happening. There are other villages far from here. We could run. Hide. It would keep you safe."

I hadn't volunteered for the hunt like my sister had one year ago. No, they'd shoved me, a widow, to the top of the list, and when the two names were announced in the village square, mine was spoken first.

"I don't mind," I said, packing the rest of my few belongings. My deceased husband, dear man though he was, had not possessed much, and I'd come to our marriage with even less. "Actually, I almost welcome leaving the memories of Sveth behind. I see him every-where. I hear his voice right behind me, calling to me. Yet when I turn, he's not there." It shattered me each time.

"Better to face a ghost of someone you loved than lie beneath a rutting orc," Kael snarled.

One male rutting was pretty much the same as the next, wasn't it? Not that I had much experience, just that of my husband. After the initial pain, the rutting wasn't terrible. Sveth hadn't pushed me for relations more than once a week. Perhaps if he had, I might've been with child when he got sick and died. At least then, I'd have a memory of him to hold close.

Instead, my arms remained empty.

"There's nothing for me here any longer except for you, dear friend," I said. If Kael hadn't taken me in after Sveth died, I wasn't sure what might've happened to me. Sveth's home was claimed by his family who hadn't held me in high regard. Women cannot own property, they'd claimed. Kael spoke up for me, but our evil mayor, Eamon, had insisted I must leave the home I'd only lived in for two months. "I'll miss you horribly, but this is for the best. Someone needs to go. Why not me?"

"No woman should have to contemplate a future with an orc."

"I'm not afraid," I said, though even I could hear the

tremor in my voice. "Remember, my sister said the orcs are kind."

Kael drew himself up, crossing his arms on his chest. "I'm not convinced."

"The decision has been made." I flung the strap of my bag over my shoulder, and none too soon.

Eamon banged on the door. "Time to leave. The sun has set. The orcs wait."

"He takes too much pleasure in this," Kael said softly.

I dropped my bag and hugged him. This was likely the last time I'd see him. Rhoslyn's orc mate had brought her to visit me months ago, but I doubted anyone would bring me here to visit Kael.

"Take care, friend," I said. "Thank you for all you've done for me."

"*You* take care," he said. "You're the one who needs it most."

He followed me from his small home. As I passed through the solemn crowd who'd gathered to witness our sacrifice, a few touched my arms, wishing me well. Most watched with relief in their eyes. For this year, *they* were safe.

Alwen stood with her mother beside the gate. When she heard me approaching, she turned her steely gaze my way. Some villagers scorned her, because she wore pants like a male, and she hunted, something no other women did. If anyone could escape the orcs and find a way to survive in the forest, it would be her.

I nodded as I passed her and took the bag waiting for

me beside the gate. They were packed for those chosen, and while the clothing would be too loose on my lean frame, I wouldn't turn down the chance for a few more outfits. Only the fates knew when I'd be offered more.

"Shall we walk together?" I asked Alwen, who nodded grimly. "Perhaps we can protect each other." Though I doubted even she'd be much good against a fearsome orc. At nearly twice our size, any of them could knock us to the ground with one blow if they wanted.

Only when I contemplated what was about to happen did my heart freeze. Could I remain strong and hold back my shrieks when an orc claimed me?

It appeared I was about to find out.

With a nod to Kael and Alwen's mother, I walked with Alwen to the gate and through the tiny opening the guards created to allow us to pass.

We hurried across the big open stretch of grass between the village's high fortress walls and the forest. My heart thudded too quickly in my ears, and my breathing came out overly loud, ragged.

"Stay close with me, and you might just survive this," Alwen whispered. Her hand went to the knife sheathed at her side. "I have a weapon, and I'm not afraid to use it." She pulled it, brandishing it with a feral look in her eyes.

A chitter echoed from the forest. Damn, there were shaydes nearby. They hunted at night, and we would soon be their prey. Would it be better to be killed by one of them or lie beneath a rutting orc?

I swallowed deeply, but I couldn't get anything past the lump of terror in my throat.

We entered the woods, leaving the relative safety of the moonlit field behind.

Guttural cries rang out somewhere in the distance.

Alwen shot me a dark look and nodded. "Remember. Stay with me. Don't fall behind." She bolted into the woods, and I started after her, but she was much too fast, and I soon lost her in the dark.

I slowed my pace. Better to take care where I placed my feet than stomp around and draw attention.

An orc would claim me whether I ran, walked, or laid on the ground and waited for him to arrive.

I didn't care one bit how it came about.

It wasn't like I had anything left to live for.

CHAPTER 2

MADR

I was going to be late for the mate hunt, and it was my father's fault. He'd come to my home in the mountains and told me I was not allowed to participate in the hunt.

A snarl ripped through me. How dare he try to tell me what to do? "You have no say in this matter."

"How could you bear to lie with a human?" he sneered.

"I want a mate. This is a chance to have one." I struggled to remain patient. This male was not only my father but the king of the orc kingdom. Just because I'd scorned him, abdicating my role as prince and his heir, and walked from his palace never to return, didn't mean I could treat him any differently than other citizens of the kingdom. I needed to respect his role as king even if I couldn't respect him.

"I can parade a large number of eligible orc females past you. Your pendant will flare for one of them."

I wrapped my hand around my Lumen Clan pendant, the spikes from the sun symbol digging into my palm. "It has just as much chance of blazing for a human."

He scoffed. "I understand why some would choose to mate with a female this way. I'm not opposed to our males mating with them in general. But they're homely. Fragile. They'll break if an orc tried to mate with them."

"Jaus's mate, Rhoslyn wouldn't agree. Their lovely daughter, your only grandchild, Shirra, would also disagree about a human's ability to mate with an orc."

"What's she like?" he asked, his golden gaze softening. He tugged on his black hair shot through with green much like my own. I'd inherited my green eyes from my now deceased mother. She, like many of our females, was killed during a coordinated shayde attack.

My father changed after her death. Sometimes, I felt as if I'd lost both of my parents that day. My father might as well have buried himself with her in the grave.

"Shirra's adorable," I said, my heart warming instantly. "A bit of them both. She has Jaus's berry-streaked black hair but Rhoslyn's blue eyes. She's a lovely mix of orc and human, and you're missing out on so much by not making time for her in your life. Go see her. Tell Jaus you accept him as your son—"

My father growled.

Why was he stubborn about this? Everyone knew

Jaus was his, even my half-brother. My father had shoved Jaus's mother aside when he met mine. He'd mated Mother, but he'd already produced Jaus. My mother discovered Jaus's existence within a year of my birth and encouraged us to spend time together. I loved my brother and knew how it saddened him that our father refused to accept him.

"Or don't accept Jaus," I said in a reasonable tone I had to struggle to project. "Visit them. Smile if you're capable of it. Meet Shirra. Hold her. A child can change everything." She might even soften my father. "She's a sweet orcling. Happy and incredibly smart."

The longing in my father's eyes was like a kick in the belly. Perhaps he'd finally realized all he'd missed out on by locking his heart away after Mother's death.

"I cannot," he said softly.

"You're much too stubborn." I held up my hand when he grumbled. "I'm sure I get it from you. Mother was sweet and kind and so eager to please others."

"She was the best life had to offer." He pinched his eyes shut but for only a moment.

"Do what you will. I must leave or I'll miss the hunt." Turning away from him, I grabbed my flail from where I'd left it standing in the corner near the front door. When I battled dresalods or shaydes, I attached a chain with a mace to the top, but for tonight, I'd take the simple pole with me for the hunt. I was equally good at fighting without the mace, and I doubted I'd need to defend a mate. The odds of the fates choosing one for me over all the other worthy orcs was slim. "I'll see you when I return?"

It wasn't polite for me to leave before the king, but if I remained here much longer, I'd arrive long after the two women were claimed. The fates might have me in mind for one of them, but if I wasn't there, they might pick another.

My heart surged into my throat. Would I find the joy I'd sought for most of my life or would I return home in a few days, my soul wallowing in disappointment? Only to try again next year and the one after that, until I was too old to please a mate.

The king sighed and strode around me, pretending he'd chosen to leave first. Pride meant everything to him. Too much, in fact. It had already been his downfall.

He left without saying anything further, but what else could I expect? When he scorned my half-brother Jaus for the final time, adding to the insult by mocking Rhoslyn, I'd had enough. I told him we were done, that he could keep his crown forever or hand it to a shayde for all I cared. I'd stormed from his palace and hadn't returned. I couldn't allow anyone to treat my family with that much disrespect, not even a king.

Rhoslyn was amazing. If only I could find a female just like her.

My winged vox, Brakkis, waited for me behind my home, and I leaped up onto his spine. A nudge of my heels and he sprung into flight, his wings snapping out to catch the wind.

When orcs reached maturity, we traveled to the desert Ember Clan, the caretakers of these mighty beasts.

Voxes formed within a seed half the size of an orc, and when they slipped out, they bonded with the orc closest to them. We worked with them as they matured, which took about a year, and when they were ready for flight, we trained them in that as well. They remained close to us after that, nesting in trees and high in the mountains, only returning to the Ember Clan when it was time to mate, something they did every three years.

Brakkis's golden scales gleamed in the late-day sunlight as I guided him over the orc city. Most of the silver buildings spiked up three stories, their smooth metal sides a deterrent to the clawed dresalods who attacked from the sea beyond the high city walls.

We soared through the pass in the mountains and flew out over the vast forest that stretched from here all the way around and beyond the human village I sought.

It took me two nights' travel to reach the village. I stopped only to sleep a bit during the day. Shaydes preferred to hunt at night, though I still lit a fire for protection while I rested.

By the time I landed Brakkis in an open meadow with the other voxes, night was in full force and bonded males either hunted one of the two village women or were making their way back to their voxes to fly home.

I was late. Too late to match with a mate?

Then my clan pendant flared brighter than a star fallen from the sky.

The only reason I didn't shout out my joy was because I didn't want to draw the attention of shaydes.

My mate was one of the two women.

Now I needed to track her down and claim her.

CHAPTER 3
LYNETH

Telling myself I was going to walk, not run, through the woods was all well and good until a shayde's chitter rang out from my right, followed by the hoots of what I took for orcs.

Both hunted me.

My heart roared up into my throat, making it almost impossible to breathe. I bolted forward, rushing along the path, my footsteps making too much noise in the dry leaves coating the forest floor.

Stomps rang out from my right, followed by a chitter. Damn, I didn't need to worry about being rutted by an orc. I was going to be eaten alive by a shayde, just like my parents were when I was thirteen.

Only now did I wish I'd gotten a second chance. Maybe not at love. I'd adored my husband. But it would've been nice to have someone kind to talk with. To sit with on a porch. To have children with.

I couldn't give up yet. Spying a thick tree ahead with branches low enough I just might reach, I raced toward it. Leaping, I grabbed the branch. I'd climbed every tree in the village when I was little. My muscles may have forgotten the way, but my mind and will still knew how to do it.

I swung my leg over the branch and levered myself up until I lay on my belly. This was an undignified way to climb, but I wasn't complaining. As far as I knew, shaydes couldn't scale trees.

Another branch was within my reach, and I did the same, grabbing onto it and pulling myself up. Just in time.

I froze when a shayde stalked beneath me, swinging its head back and forth, its glowing red eyes seeking prey. The enormous, four-legged lizard lifted its nose as if it caught my scent, and it paused, snapping its fangs. Moonlight gleamed on its scaly hide.

It rose onto its back legs, revealing its pale brown underbelly, its snout lifting. I held my breath and clung to the tree, hoping it wouldn't pick me out among the leafy branches above.

When it dropped down onto its front legs again and moved forward, its long tail sweeping back and forth, I carefully pulled in a breath and released it. My muscles twitched from spent adrenaline, and it was all I could do to reach for another branch. I'd keep climbing as high as I could and when I found a safe place, I'd remain there until morning.

No one had ever returned from the hunt, but perhaps I could be the first. Would they kick me out, tell me I needed to wander the forest until an orc claimed me? Or would they welcome me back in the morning with open arms?

For all I knew, this would spoil the treaty.

I'd worry about that tomorrow.

I was scrambling to stand on another branch when an odd sound caught my attention. Rising to my feet, I turned.

Orcs surrounded me, some sitting on the branches of nearby trees, others standing close enough I could reach out and touch them.

They watched me, and if orcs could appear stunned, these ones did. One gaped at me, his jaw dropping.

Another leered.

All of them advanced toward me.

I yelped and let go of the trunk, backing out onto the branch. A glance behind told me I couldn't go far before the limb would snap.

"I claim you in the name of the Lumen Clan," the leering one snarled.

"That won't be necessary," a soft voice said from below. The orc leaped and grabbed onto the branch I precariously perched on. He easily swung himself up to stand. He stood at least three heads taller than me and was twice as broad.

The pendant on his chest blazed like a star in the darkest night.

"You have no say in this, Madr," the one who'd "claimed" me declared. "Go. She's mine."

"My Lumen pendant says otherwise, Riank. I note yours isn't blazing."

I didn't know much about orcs, but even I could hear the sound of death ringing in Madr's voice.

"You're nothing now, *cousin*," Riank said. "A mere citizen of the kingdom. With you out of my way, I'll rule when your father's gone. May that day come soon."

Snarling, Madr leaped onto Riank.

The two males toppled off the tree, falling toward the ground.

CHAPTER 4

MADR

R iank and I twisted and battled even as we fell from the top of the tree. My hip hit a branch, my arm another, and I bit back groans. We crashed into the dense underbrush in a tangle of smacking limbs and throaty growls. My heart pounded, and I sucked in a deep breath, springing away from him and onto my feet.

Orcs leaped to the ground from above, landing lightly around us. They'd bear witness to our battle, though they knew as well as me that my pendant had chosen the female, not his.

The moon's pale light bathed the forest floor as my cousin Riank jumped to his feet. He yanked his short sword from the sheath on his back as I pulled my flail.

We circled each other, him gouging his blade my way, me deflecting it easily with my staff. I'd been trained to use many weapons by the best the kingdom had to offer. My father would never raise a soft prince.

Riank's eyes gleamed with a feral rage.

"Feeling fortunate tonight?" he asked, his attention falling on my pendant that no longer glowed. "We merely saw a reflection of the moonlight. Our clan did not choose her for you." He slammed forward, stabbing with his blade, but I darted to the side and smacked down hard on his hand with my flail.

His sword wavered in his grip, but he tightened his hand on it and snarled.

"You know what we all saw," I said, watching for another chance to end this. While I held no love for my conniving cousin, that didn't mean I wanted to kill him. "She's mine."

"Not unless you can take her from me."

We circled each other, our eyes locked in an intense stare. The smell of damp earth and the musky stench of his sweat hung heavy in the air. My senses were heightened, and every rustling leaf, every whisper of the wind, was amplified.

Riank lunged at me with his sword, aiming to deliver a swift and deadly blow. I deftly sidestepped his attack, my staff whirling through the air, seeking to knock him off balance. The clashing of our weapons reverberated through the forest, making the birds and insects around us still. They listened.

As did shaydes. One chittered in the distance, and if

we didn't end this fast, we'd be battling it in addition to each other.

"You've always been weak," he spat, his words laced with malice. "Abandoning your birthright, running from your destiny. You're nothing but a pitiful disgrace."

My blood boiled, but I refused to give into my rage. That was his intention, to make me angry so I'd act instead of thinking about how to make my best move first.

He snarled when he realized I wouldn't take his bait.

We battled on, our weapons a blur of motion illuminated by the moon's glow. The clash of our weapons and our grunts of exertion filled my ears. The earthy aroma of the forest lifted from the leaves rustling under our feet.

Seeing an opening, I swept out my flail, hitting his hand hard enough to send his sword soaring through the night. A second blow to his chest made him stumble backward. I pressed him against a tree, holding the tip of my staff firmly against his throat.

"Yield," I growled, pressing hard.

His breath wheezed and his eyes filled with rage. "Never."

"Yield now or you won't be given another chance."

His head jerked in a nod, and I suspected this was the only concession he'd make.

I backed away and after sheathing my flail, I climbed toward my mate.

I'd have to start watching my back long before my cousin took rule of the kingdom.

CHAPTER 5
LYNETH

If one of the orcs hadn't grabbed my arm and held me in place, I would've climbed down the tree and fled into the forest despite my fear of the shaydes.

"Release me," I snarled, trying to wrench away.

He chuckled and watched the drama unfolding on the forest floor.

Since I couldn't escape the orc's grip, I watched as well.

"Madr fights for you," the orc said. "You should be honored."

I sniffed but said nothing.

My fingers gripping the rough bark, I held my breath as the battle continued.

The two towering orcs circled each other, each watching for an opening they'd use to their advantage.

Madr held a staff, which surely couldn't compete with a sword.

"The metal blade will slice right through his staff," I whispered. "He'll lose."

I couldn't understand why I wanted him to win. It shouldn't matter to me which orc claimed me. Rutted with me.

I couldn't understand their words because they spoke in low, guttural voices.

My heart pounded against my ribcage, and an inexplicable mix of excitement and worry coursed through me, though I didn't know exactly what I feared.

"Madr will make short work of his cousin," the orc beside me said. "Riank may hold a sword, but he rarely trained. I imagine he's regretting that decision."

An undeniable power emanated from Madr, as if he were channeling the essence of the world around us. Every swing of his thick staff sent shockwaves through the air.

The clash of their weapons echoed in the clearing. Madr moved with grace, surprisingly fast for his enormous size. Each swing of his staff was like a choreographed dance, a display of skill that left me amaze, though I knew almost nothing about weapons or battle.

When Madr disarmed Riank and forced him to yield, an overwhelming desire washed over me, confusing my thoughts. I had no interest in being with an orc, yet I found myself unable to look away. There was something captivating about Madr, something beyond his physical prowess. It was as if his inner fire burned brighter than any I'd encountered before.

As he sheathed his staff and sprang upward, moving toward me, the orc holding me in place leaped to another tree. He dropped to the ground and moved swiftly through the forest until he disappeared from view.

Madr planted his feet on the thick branch beside me. He shot me a grin that came out almost boyish. For whatever reason, it made me long to soften inside. But I couldn't. I *wouldn't*. That would betray not only my dead husband but my very soul.

His pendant blazed brightly as if it had a heart of its own.

Madr's startling green eyes met mine. "I, Madr Thourand, claim you in the name of the Lumen Clan."

CHAPTER 6
MADR

I nodded to Yevest, who'd remained protectively with my mate while I was unable to do so. He was a member of the Azuris Clan like my half-brother Jaus.

Yevest grunted, and while envy lurked in his eyes, he only nodded to the woman and me, then leaped off the tree, landing squarely on the ground. At a jog, he soon disappeared quickly into the vegetation, heading toward where he'd left his vox. Like I'd had to return to the hunt year after year, so would he. He was a decent male. I wished him luck next year.

After I claimed her, my mate studied me. I was surprised not to find fear in her eyes. Did I see resignation? Perhaps.

"As I said, I'm Madr," I grunted, unsure how to speak with a woman. Such a strange feeling. I could easily converse with Rhoslyn. Why not this one? "What's your name?"

My mate was gorgeous from her golden hair and blue eyes common among her people to her slender frame.

"I'm Lyneth." She drew her body up stiffly. "Are you going to rut with me now?"

I tilted my head, watching her face, but she still didn't appear frightened. "Would you like me to?"

She blinked. "I find myself at a loss because I've heard varying stories about orcs, and I'm not sure what to believe. Some say you're brutal beasts who strip the bones off a child's limbs with your tusks."

"I've yet to eat a child," I said solemnly. Humor bubbled up inside me. My mate was a delight already.

"That has yet to be seen. Someone else told me orcs are kind and can be trusted, though I have my doubts."

"Perhaps you'd prefer to get to know me better before you decide?"

"Perhaps."

I held out my hand. "Come with me. I'll take you to my home. Over time, you'll be able to decide if I nibble on children or . . . pretty little mates."

Color rose in her cheeks, followed by fury in her eyes. "Don't be nice to me," she snapped.

"Why not?" I kept my hand extended, though she hadn't taken it. Other males might've grabbed her and leaped from the tree. Not me. I was patient, if nothing else.

"Because it will have no effect on my emotions. My heart belongs to another."

"That could be a problem. Where is this . . . other?" I pretended to look around, but I didn't need to. I'd already scanned the area, noting everyone had left for their voxes. I'd keep an eye out for Riank, though I doubted he'd attack me so soon after his witnessed defeat. No, he'd bide his time and wait for a better opportunity, one where he could eliminate me without anyone realizing he was the person who'd done it.

"My beloved Sveth is dead."

"You were mated with another." To my surprise, jealousy churned through me. I'd just met Lyneth. I had no reason to feel this way, especially about someone who'd died.

"I was."

One or two orcs may have ignored the fact that her heart belonged to another. They would've taken her to their homes and within days, rutted with her. But that had only happened in the first season or two of the hunt. This must be where the rumors had come from. Eleven years had passed since then, and after twenty-two women mating successfully with orcs, my species had learned to be patient. A mate would come around if given the chance.

"I have time to woo you, tiny female," I said softly, my hand dropping to my side.

"You'll find I'm not easily wooed."

"A challenge?" I was more than ready. My clan's

pendant had chosen her, which meant she was the one I'd adore until my dying day. Jaus and Rhoslyn hadn't loved each other from the start.

A prize one had to work for was worth much more than something easily given.

"Will you remain here in the tree?" I asked.

Panic flashed through her eyes. "You're leaving me?"

"Why would I do such a thing?"

"Because I told you I won't willingly mate with you."

"I'd never take you if you weren't willing, but you will be."

She snorted. "Is this a universal thing with males?"

"What might that be, sweet?"

She rolled her eyes at my endearment, but it was appropriate. She looked delectably sweet, and her scent was intoxicating, a mix of something floral and her unique scent. I wanted to nuzzle her neck and suck in her essence while I pumped my cock inside her. "The assumption that you'll be able to somehow make me enjoy your rutting." Her scornful gaze traveled up and down my frame.

"You stated you loved another."

"I did."

"Then you understand the pleasure that can be found in the sexual act."

A frown crossed her face. "My Sveth did enjoy the act."

"And you?"

"Women don't . . ."

"Don't enjoy sex? Why would you think that?"

"Because that's how it is."

"In that, you're wrong, sweet, and I'll soon show you." My heart surged with excitement. She'd loved another but hadn't found pleasure with him?

I could work with this.

CHAPTER 7

LYNETH

Madr was highly appealing from his broad, muscular frame to his dark hair woven through with a sage green, to his forest-colored eyes.

Did all orcs wear only a scrap of leather bound around their waist and groin? I noted a large bulge beneath the front and quickly yanked my gaze away, not wanting to do anything that might make his cock respond. While I hadn't found pleasure in the sexual act, I hadn't minded when Sveth did it, because he'd hold me after and tell me how much he cared.

Madr was much too cocky, assuming I'd somehow enjoy his rutting. Let him try. He'd soon discover I was like every other female in that aspect.

"Where do you plan to take me?" I asked.

"To the orc city, though I live in the mountains nearby, not within the city itself."

Rhoslyn lived in the city. I'd be very close!

"I'll go with you for now." Once I was near Rhoslyn, I'd find a way to escape. If I begged her for sanctuary, surely, she wouldn't insist I remain with this . . . orc.

His thick brow drew together. "Very well."

Before I could contemplate what might happen next, he'd tugged me against his chest. A boost, and he laid me over his shoulder.

Yelping, I flailed, my legs spiraling and my hands smacking onto his naked back. His greenish-gold skin was warm and smoother than I thought it would be. It almost felt nice, a silly, random thought.

"Hold on," Madr said, pivoting on the branch. He leaped, and my stomach flipped over as we dropped to the ground. He landed squarely and lowered me to my feet.

"I . . . I . . ." I wasn't sure what to say. "How did you do that?"

"Do what?" He took my hand and tugged me toward the woods, holding his staff in his other hand. His gaze scanned the area for threats.

I felt safe with this orc who'd already proven his skills in battle. At least the fates had been good enough to pair me with someone who could protect me until I could find a way to my sister.

With the moon lighting our way, we traveled swiftly through the forest, following a trail I didn't see until he placed his feet on it. He held onto my hand as if he was worried I'd bolt.

"I won't run away from you," I said. Not yet, that is.

He paused and held up his hand, his gaze sweeping the woods around us. Finally, his arm lowered, and he leaned close, speaking by my ear. "Don't talk. We don't want to draw attention."

Shaydes. I was a fool for forgetting.

When I nodded, he flashed his tusks my way.

His smile was as gorgeous as he was, and I didn't like the swimming feeling his attention gave me.

He kissed my cheek, and I didn't like that either. I was a widow. You'd think a random kiss wouldn't make me feel like leaning into his chest.

I stepped away from him, also not enjoying how my heartrate picked up with him nearby. I was frightened of him; that was all it was.

But as I followed him through the forest, I knew that was a lie.

For some reason, I found this orc appealing, and that felt like a betrayal of Sveth. Would he have wanted me to find someone new? We'd never discussed such a thing. We wed and within months, he was sick and then gone.

I swallowed hard against the lump of pain in my throat. It hurt to think we'd never grow old together, never have children.

Madr stopped ahead of me so fast, I ran into his back. My hands went to his hips to maintain my balance, and as if a tiny lightning bolt shot through me, my skin flared with heat.

I stepped away from him, staring at my hands that betrayed me.

Madr released a guttural cry. He latched onto my arm and tugged me behind him as he rushed out into a small meadow and crossed it.

When he stopped and released me, I gaped at the enormous creature resting on its haunches in the deep grass. Its scales gleamed like gold in the moonlight, and it was at least three times Madr's size. Shaped a bit like a lizard, it had wings tucked against its sides, a long tail, and spikes marching from the top of its head to its shoulders, though those near its head were much shorter. It turned its long snout our way, its nostrils flaring.

Dark liquid trickled down its side from one of its wings.

Its gaze fell on me, and for a moment, I remained frozen, convinced it would rip through me with its fangs or smash me with its big, clawed feet.

Self-preservation kicked in. Gasping, I backed away while Madre continued to surge forward. The creature didn't attack when he stopped in front of it and cupped its cheeks.

"Brakkis," he said softly, stroking the beast's face. "What did he do to you?"

While he moved from Brakkis's head around to the creature's side, I crept forward, though I kept distance between us.

"You know this . . . Brakkis," I whispered.

"I raised him from the time he slipped from his seed,"

Madr said sadly. "Don't be frightened. He'd never hurt you." He carefully extended one of Brakkis's wings. Blood seeped from a stab wound that had punctured through the creature's limb.

The feral gaze Madr sent my way made a shudder rip through me.

"I'll kill him for this," he snarled.

"You speak of the male you fought?" I moved closer, keeping Madr between me and Brakkis. The beast might be friendly with him, but that didn't mean it wouldn't kill me.

"My cousin, Riank, has a nasty way of getting even." He turned his full gaze my way. "Brakkis will not be able to fly."

"Fly?" I felt foolish for repeating him. "You actually . . . ride Brakkis?"

"It took us two nights of flying to reach this part of the forest."

My sister was that far away? "Can't we walk?"

He shook his head. "It would take too long and it's much too dangerous. Shaydes would get us in no time."

"You'd protect me."

"I appreciate your confidence in me, but I cannot fight all of them."

"I can return to the village," I said with a lift of my chin.

"That's not an option, mate."

That's right. I was his mate. Or he believed it was so. I wasn't convinced. But in that, he was correct. Returning wasn't an option. The villagers wouldn't let me back inside the fortress. They'd remind me I was a gift to the orcs in exchange for their protection. And this orc was more than willing to claim me to fulfill the treaty.

"What will we do?" I asked, my heart twisting. My plan was unraveling at the seams in front of my eyes.

"We'll remain here until his wing has healed."

CHAPTER 8

MADR

To think my cousin would take his anger out on a vox. They were gentle, sweet creatures.

But this was more than about revenge. Brakkis couldn't fly with a wound like this. It would take days to heal, and that would keep me pinned to the ground where the shaydes would find me.

He was next in line for the throne, and he knew that while I'd abdicated my role as prince, my father had yet to announce who'd take my place on the throne after he passed.

If I was dead, the elders might insist my father name Riank his heir.

Taking a small jar of healing ointment from the pouch I'd left hooked to one of his spikes, I generously slathered it over both sides of the wound. He groaned softly as the pain eased.

"A few days, friend," I said, holding his face and

stroking his cheeks. "That will give you time to heal." Stepping back, I waved for my mate to come closer. "Remain near my vox."

Lyneth looked from me to Brakkis. "It won't eat me?"

"No, sweet, voxes don't consume meat. If anyone eats you, it will be me." I wasn't sure why I kept poking her about this. Maybe because I couldn't stop thinking about the fact that she believed women didn't find pleasure in sex. The notion made my cock stir and my pulse jump to double time. I wanted to show her how very wrong she was about that.

Was it sick of me to take joy in the fact that she was still innocent despite having been with another?

"You told me orcs don't strip a child's bones with their tusks," she said.

I moved closer to her, sucking in her heady scent once more. "We don't."

She crossed her arms on her chest and looked up at me defiantly. "Then don't taunt me with threats of killing and eating me."

"Oh, your body is completely safe with me, mate." I leaned even closer, and when she didn't back away, I ran my tongue across her earlobe. "There are parts of your body I look forward to stroking in just this way. *This* is what I mean by eating you."

She backed up and swatted her hand between us like I was a teetser who'd buzzed in for a bite. "I can't imagine why anyone would find pleasure in someone licking their ear."

"It won't be your ear I'll be after." It was going to be so much fun awakening my new mate sexually. Perhaps the way to do this would be through teasing. "There's a place between your legs that will welcome my tongue."

She gasped as if scandalized. "I don't believe you."

"Is that a dare?"

Sputtering, she shook her head. "It's not true. It can't be."

"Tell you what," I said. "The first thing I need to do is collect enough wood for a large fire. That'll keep shaydes away. Then we'll eat and drink the provisions I brought with me." I'd have to hunt soon and collect more water, but I had enough for a few days.

"What does all that have to do with your tongue and . . ." She shakily glanced down at her body.

I grinned. "After we've eaten and when I'm confident we're safe, I'll show you if you'd like. I'll never force you to do anything you're uncomfortable with."

"You expect me to expose my private areas to you?"

"Only long enough for me to prove to you that licking one secret spot will bring you pleasure."

He was lying. There was no secret spot between my legs that would give me pleasure.

"I suspect you're daring me," I said. "Telling a story to tease me."

"Oh, I am daring you, sweet. I am." He flashed a tusk-filled grin my way that made heat swirl through me. I ached . . . between my legs. Was that the area he spoke of? I shrugged off the idea. It wasn't true, and we'd soon prove he was a liar.

"I'll help you collect wood." There was no need for me to remain near his vox when there was work to do.

"All right, thank you."

We walked around the nearby woods, him so quietly, I wouldn't know he was there if I couldn't see him in the dim light, while I was doing my best not to make a huge racket. After collecting a large pile of wood, he stooped down and dug a shallow circle in the ground, exposing the dirt, then ringed it with rocks I also helped him collect.

In no time, a fire blazed merrily, and I had to admit, it brought comfort.

"I trust you," I said.

He looked at me where I stood beside him. With him resting on his heels, we were eye level, reminding me again how much bigger he was than me. "I appreciate that." Humor shone in his voice and eyes.

"It's not funny."

The humor dropped away in an instant. "I'll try my best not to do anything that betrays that trust."

"Like your cousin. He attacked your vox." I glanced at the big creature resting more comfortably on his side, though his sharp eyes scanned the area, and his ears flicked in all directions to detect sounds.

"He was getting even with me for defeating him in battle."

"I can't imagine having family and not wishing them well."

"Brakkis knows Riank. My cousin took advantage of that trust. I doubt he even had to sneak up on Brakkis. My vox would allow him to come near, never suspecting Riank would cause harm."

"Your cousin is mean."

"He won't stop until I'm dead."

I gasped. "He'd kill you because of . . . me?" I couldn't believe mates were so valuable that one orc would attack another for possession.

"He wanted you. They all did. But the rest know our clan pendants choose, not them." He cupped the sun-shaped pendant dangling on his chest before releasing it.

"A pendant can't choose a mate for anyone," I scoffed.

"And yet, mine did. Surely you saw it blazing."

As if it heard him, it flashed light, quickly winking out.

"That's . . . That's . . ." This couldn't be possible. "It's the moon's reflection, nothing else."

One side of his mouth quirked up. "Believe what you will. I'll continue to trust the fates who told me you're my mate." He rose and grabbed the pouch lying on the ground nearby. "Sit. We'll eat and have something to drink."

"And then you'll show me a secret place between my legs?" I said sarcastically. I didn't know why I continued to poke him verbally. Part of me had the odd urge to get close enough to him that our skin would touch, while the rest of me insisted I wanted nothing to do with this orc.

"If you wish."

I crossed my arms on my chest. "Why would I wish for something like that?"

"Curiosity is a powerful thing." He patted the ground beside him. "Sit."

I took a few steps back from him and sat there.

He grunted and opened the pouch, pulling out a large clump of something wrapped in waxed fabric. Unwrapping it, he revealed chunks made up of berries, nuts, seeds, and some kind of paste holding it all together.

My belly rumbled, and his lips twitched.

"Here you are." He held out a chunk, though he didn't extend his arm far enough for me to reach.

Grumbling, I scooted closer to him and took the piece, nibbling on it.

"You're welcome," he said, biting into a chunk himself.

My cheeks blazed, and I squirmed. "Thank you. I don't mean to be rude."

"You're just unsettled, and your feelings are coming through in your words and actions. I don't blame you one bit. If I was in your position, I'd be nervous as well."

"I'm not nervous." My words came out full of defiance, but inside, I knew he was right. My belly quaked and it had nothing to do with hunger.

"Fearful, then."

"Not that either."

He flashed me a smile. "Then you must be excited about what I might do with your body."

I gasped. "Never that."

"Never is a very long time, sweet."

"Don't call me that. I have a proper name, Lyneth."

"You seem so very sweet."

My huff rang out. "I'm anything but that."

"That's a matter of perspective."

"It doesn't' matter. I know my mind and heart. It won't be changed."

"Perhaps a time will come when I'll call you on that." He nudged his chin to a flask lying between us. "Drink well. I'll refill it at the river later."

He must mean the one weaving across the open area beyond the fortress walls. While some of the wealthy had water brought into their homes by pipes, something I could barely dream of, the rest of us carried buckets.

"Will we sleep near the fire tonight?" I asked, peering into the woods. Nothing moved, but that didn't mean a shayde wasn't watching. A shiver burst across my skin, and I leaned near the flames.

"The fire is to protect Brakkis."

"Will Brakkis protect me from you?"

His lips curled up and there went those odd flips through my belly. "My vox is loyal to me above all others."

Figured.

"We could seek shelter in the village," I said.

He scoffed. "You believe they'd welcome an orc among them?"

"If you were polite and promised to behave yourself, I'm sure they'd give you sanctuary. Humans are not cruel." Not overly much, that is.

"It has nothing to do with whether they'd be kind to me or not. We protect your people from the shaydes in exchange for two humans per year. The last thing we'd wish to do is imply we need *your* protection." His smile rose again. "There's one thing you need to know about me, mate."

"What's that?"

"I *never* behave."

CHAPTER 10

MADR

After making sure nothing lurked in the area, though Brakkis would sound the alarm long before I saw or heard anything approaching, I nudged my chin toward my mate.

"Come. We'll go to the river for water."

"I could wait here with Brakkis."

"Is that what you wish to do?"

She shrugged.

"We'll also bathe," I said.

Her chin lifted. "Maybe I'm not interested in bathing."

"You stink." She didn't, but I appeared to enjoy irking her and couldn't resist saying it.

Rising to her feet, she stomped her foot on the ground. "I do not stink."

"Orcs have an incredible sense of smell. From where I'm standing, you do."

"Then remain far away from me."

"How will I show you that secret place that gives you pleasure if I do something like that?" Would she call my dare or find a way to back out of this?

"I've told you such a place does not exist. If one did, I would've discovered it myself or heard about it from the other women." She trooped over to her bag and rifled inside it, pulling out clean clothing. Glaring my way, she huffed and started walking toward the woods.

"Where are you going?" I asked, though I kept my voice low.

"To the river."

I lifted my arm. "It's in that direction."

She pivoted and stalked back to me, passing me and continuing to the woods. "I assume there's some sort of path I can follow?"

With a grin, I caught up to her and took her hand. "I'll happily lead you, sweet." I wasn't sure why I felt so sunny when she was incredibly cranky, but I enjoyed our verbal sparring.

She rolled her eyes but didn't tug away. "Hardly sweet if I stink."

I chuckled.

With my flail in hand for possible defense and my pack on my back, I led her through the forest, periodically pausing to listen. The shaydes must be hunting elsewhere because I didn't hear or sense any nearby.

It would be unwise to drop my guard, however. After they attacked the orc city all at once, killing most of our women we'd hidden in what we believed was a safe location, we'd decimated the shayde population. The vengeance felt good, but it would never bring back the women we'd all adored.

I'd lost my mother in the raid, and my father had never been the same. The anger that she'd restrained with her gentle touch was unleashed, and he too often directed his ire at me. I'd learned to avoid him until I was grown, and when he snapped yet another time—in this instance directing his rage toward my half-brother Jaus and his new mate—I'd snapped myself and told my father I no longer wanted anything to do with him.

He'd yet to accept this, but he would. I was as stubborn as him in this regard.

We reached the river, and I stopped, studying the glassy water. Broad, the river churned a bit in the center, telling me that was where it was deepest and where the current flowed fastest.

"Do you have a river where you live for bathing?" she asked, lowering her clothing to the ground.

"I bathe in the room adjacent to my bedroom."

"I'm surprised."

"That orcs are civilized enough to have running water and bathing chambers?"

Her shrug and the pinkening of her cheeks gave me my answer.

"You'll soon discover much about orcs, and then you'll better understand us. We have differences, obviously, but we're more alike than you realize." I couldn't drum up irritation with her for thinking we might live like animals, not when she was a product of the world she'd grown up in. I'd heard orcs were universally despised in her village. We could only change one mind at a time until the realization we were people equal to humans spread.

She sniffed.

"Can you swim?" I asked.

"Yes."

"Very well." I loosened the tie to my loincloth, my only item of clothing.

"Wait," she said with a frown, her gaze locked on my fingers. "What are you doing?"

"I bathe naked, don't you?"

"I wash in my room with water from a bucket. I'm naked there, naturally, but alone."

"You said you can swim."

"I've done so during the warm months but only with other women. Never with a male present."

"Would you like me to leave you here where the shaydes can find you just to give you a moment alone to bathe?"

"You can't. We . . ." She huffed. "Turn away, then. Do not look at my body."

My low laugh rang out. "There will come a time when you'll enjoy my touch and warm gaze, sweet."

"I cannot ever see anything like that happening."

"The other women said the same thing after they

were claimed during the hunt, and they universally love their mates now. Many have produced orclings."

"This I have a hard time believing."

"That they'd have children?"

"That they'd universally love their orc mates."

"You'll see."

"No matter. This universal farce doesn't mean I wish for you to look upon my body at this time. Turn away and I'll remove my clothing. I'll enter the river and let you know when I'm suitably covered."

"You're so prim and proper, mate."

"As I should be."

I turned. It was useless to argue with her. Soon, we'd be in the water together, naked, and I could tease her into letting me show her how much her body would soon crave mine.

My cock wasn't as patient as me. It spiked upward, eager to be thrust inside her.

"By the fates," she said, her attention locked on my groin. "You're enormous."

"I'm no larger than any other male."

"Humans are puny in comparison."

"I feel bad for them. How do they pleasure their mates with puny cocks?" I grunted before she could speak. "That's right. They don't."

"It's not possible!"

"Are you going to remove your clothing or are we going to stand here on the shore all night arguing about something so easily proven?"

"You're incredibly irritating."

"One day, you'll enjoy how I tease you." Of this, I was completely confident. The fates and my clan pendant would not have gifted her to me if they didn't know she would love me for the rest of my days.

She rolled her eyes. "Teasing implies fun, not irking someone else."

"In this, you'll also see." I turned away and continued removing my loincloth, tossing it aside. A discrete look over my shoulder showed her gaping at my ass. It was a nice ass, muscular and with just the right amount of roundness. She could stare all she wanted.

"Are you finished?" I asked, struggling to sound completely innocent.

"Almost." Clothing rustled and fell to the ground.

My cock surged against my abdomen, and I did my best to ignore it.

She splashed into the water, releasing a low sound that made my cock ache.

"You can turn now," she whispered, wise to keep her voice low. No need to let shaydes know we were about. As far as I knew, shaydes couldn't swim, though I had no interest in testing this theory.

I faced her and savored her appreciation of my naked body. I worked out all the time—something vital for my survival. But I enjoyed battling with weapons and even running for an hour or more when I had the chance.

Now that my father no longer had me beneath his thumb, I'd joined my fellow orcs when they fought off the dresalods, though there were much fewer of them since Rhoslyn discovered a way to keep them from attacking.

"You truly are large," she said so softly, I doubted she wanted me to hear. "There's no way that thing will ever fit inside a woman. It will hurt, and it definitely won't give anyone pleasure."

Wrong. One more thing I'd soon prove beyond doubt.

Precum coated the tip of my cock, and if I was alone, I'd take care of it; deplete it right here and now. But I wasn't sure how my mate would respond to something like that. Her views on sex and satisfaction appeared to differ from an orc's.

I was going to enjoy showing my sweet Lyneth how wrong she was about that.

CHAPTER 11
LYNETH

hy was I staring at his muscular chest and shoulders that tapered to a trim waist?

Or the ripples spreading across his abdomen.

Let alone his huge cock that stood at attention like the staff he'd used to defeat his cousin.

And why was I feeling faint at the sight of it?

He frightened me, that was why. Except . . . I took pride in always being honest with myself. He didn't actually scare me. He excited me in ways I'd never felt before.

Sadly, he was soon deep enough in the water I could no longer stare at his cock.

No, I didn't wish to view it. Or touch it. My growl ripped from my throat.

Madr's head snapped around, and he peered into the woods on both sides of the river. "What do you see?" he asked softly.

Too much. "Nothing. Something brushed against my leg. A fish perhaps."

"All right." He swam toward where I floated in the middle of the river.

"There's plenty of water around us," I snapped. "You don't need to bathe near me."

He held up his hand. "Don't you want soap?"

"Oh, yes." And because I also prided myself on being kind to others, I added, "I'm sorry. I'm . . . nervous."

His low laugh tickled down my spine. "I thought you weren't nervous about me."

"It's everything." In this, I was being completely honest. "I was forced to do this. I would've been happy remaining with Kael."

"Another male?" he asked sharply, coming close enough to hand me the soap. "You said your mate died."

I lathered the soap and washed my body, handing back the soap so he could do the same. "Kael's one of the guards. He took me in after my husband died."

"Your mate didn't leave security for you when he passed?"

"His family took everything we'd collected together, stating we weren't wed long enough for me to claim it. The mayor and many in the village agreed, and that was that."

His growl rumbled through his chest. "This would never happen with orcs."

"In that, then, you're far superior."

"We're far superior in *many* ways," he said, his

humor restored. "Turn and I'll wash your hair."

"I can do that myself."

"Allow me to do this one thing for you?"

I studied his face for a long time, but it remained neutral. "All right." Turning, I presented him with my back.

"Lean back against me."

His voice sounded all growly, but I didn't think he was angry. His cock was still stiff. I could feel it shifting in the water behind me.

Perhaps he was uncomfortable. I well knew what happened when a male's cock rose. Sveth would insist I lay with him, and I'd adored him, so I hadn't minded. It was over quickly, and I could plan my activities for the rest of the day while he took care of his needs.

Since I didn't want soap in my eyes, I tipped my head back on his arm. He gently worked the lather into my hair and rinsed it, and the strokes of his fingers felt wonderful on my scalp. My skin kept tingling as he touched me, but surely that came from the cool water and not him.

When my hair was clean, he tossed the soap up onto the shore. It landed with a low thud.

I started to drop my feet to float away from him, but his arm went around my waist, holding me against his chest.

"Since you're already naked, why don't I show you that secret spot between your legs that will bring you pleasure?"

CHAPTER 12
MADR

Lyneth gulped but didn't struggle to break free.

"Assuming you're interested in learning something about your body," I added. I'd never force this, but I looked forward to awakening my mate sexually. My cock was just as eager to see her blossom.

"I still don't believe such a thing exists," she said, though weakly.

"Then you have nothing to worry about. If it doesn't exist, as you say, I promise I'll release you. I'll turn while you swim to shore, dry and dress, then you can look away while I do the same."

"You'll take my word for it?"

"Of course."

"All right. Why not?" Her low laugh rang out. "This night has been full of surprises. Let's get this over with. Then, I suppose we can be . . . friends, I guess. Nothing more."

Always more. "If you don't mind, I'll touch you in other secret spots as well."

She didn't say anything for a long moment. "Why?"

"Because I want to show you that your body can experience great pleasure."

"You want to stuff your enormous cock inside me. That's what this is about. But it's too big. It'll never fit, and I'm sure it will hurt if you try to force it."

"Which is why I won't do any such thing."

"You call me mate. Surely, you're not saying you'll live a platonic relationship with me, not with that staff between your legs rising on occasion."

I laughed, keeping it low, savoring my mate's sharp wit. "Of course I wish to do *that*, but I'll tell you what. I won't do it until you're ready, and you get to decide when it's time."

"Truly?"

"Truly."

"Then you can touch me. I dare you to prove I have secret spots that bring pleasure." The dry irony in her voice drove me on.

"You could close your eyes if you wish."

"Why would I wish to do that?"

"Because then you can block out everything else and focus on feeling."

"Hmm."

Her eyelids slid shut.

I stroked from her collarbone to beneath one of her generous breasts. I wasn't an untried orcling. It would take smooth seduction to bring her along with me, to prepare her for everything I had to offer. Grabbing her breast would reinforce her belief that her body couldn't give her pleasure.

Teasing my fingertips along the underside her breast, I floated on my back with her lying across my chest. Her legs naturally splayed apart. Perfect.

"How does this feel?" I asked, continuing to run my fingers across the smooth skin of her breast.

"I suppose it's pleasant, but no more than if you touched my arm."

Was this a challenge? I'd dealt with worse.

I guided my hand up her breast to her nipple, budded from the cool water. It was all I could do not to groan. She lay across my cock, and the movement of the water kept shifting her back and forth, back and forth. I was going to come from that alone.

I glided my thumb across her nipple slowly, circling it and tweaking the tip, before taking it between my thumb and finger and rolling it.

A moan ripped up her throat.

"Pain?" I asked, though I knew very well why she'd moaned. She might not realize it, but her hips were pumping upward, making her ass rub against my cock.

"Oh, um, no," she said, her voice shaky. "It was . . . a fish again. Brushing against my leg. You can keep doing that."

"Do you find pleasure in it?"

"I'm not sure."

"Then I need to keep doing it."

We'd floated closer to a large cluster of rocks still deep in this section. I braced my back against a boulder, and that kept us above the water and freed up my other hand. I sought her other breast and did the same thing, working toward it slowly, then focusing on the nipple. I tugged on them both, wishing more than anything that I could suck on them, stroke them with my tongue.

She was panting now, her pert lips parted. "I . . ."

"Pleasure?"

A frown knit her face. "I'm not sure."

I could hear the defiance in her voice. So she didn't want to admit that this felt good? Well, I wasn't finished with my seduction. I wasn't even close.

Leaving one breast, I stroked down across her belly.

She froze when my hand brushed across her mound.

"I promise I'll stop if you tell me to," I said. "I haven't touched your secret spot yet, however."

"Very well," she said, her voice deep and husky.

She arched her back, pushing her breast into my hand. I continued alternating tugging and rolling her nipple while my other hand stroked along her thigh in circles, slowly bringing it toward her core.

"I'm feeling something," she reluctantly admitted.

"Spread your legs apart. The spot I seek is deep between your thighs."

"That's where Sveth used to stick his cock."

The last thing I wanted to talk about was Sveth.

"I'm not him, and I'm not going to place my cock

there." Not yet, that is. "Just one or two fingers." Three if I could get away with it. "Tell me to stop if you'd like."

"You can continue."

I ran my thumb down her crease, and it slipped through fluids she'd no doubt deny. I kept rubbing slowly, dipping the tip inside with each pass.

"That doesn't seem to be the spot you've mentioned," she said. "It feels . . . all right, I suppose, but nothing earthshattering."

"Does it hurt when I touch you like this?"

"Oh, no, not at all. It . . ."

"It what?"

"I'm not sure I want to say."

"It's all right to admit you were wrong. That—"

"I'm not," she barked, settling back against my chest right away. "You don't need to stop, however. Do continue trying to prove to me that a woman can find pleasure when a male touches her body."

"I'm more than happy to do so, sweet." My cock was on fire from my seduction even if she remained impassive. But from her ragged breathing and the way she pushed her breast up into my hand, she wasn't as uninvolved as she'd like me to believe.

I slid my fingers up and down across her slit, dipping deeper inside her each time I passed her opening.

Then I placed my thumb on her clit and started rubbing.

Her groan rang out, but I didn't stop to press her to admit it felt good. I added a finger with my thumb and started rolling and tugging her clit in tandem with her nipple.

Her clit grew engorged, and despite the water, I could feel her body's response to my touch.

I continued rubbing her clit, alternating the pace between fast and hard and slow and light.

She pumped her hips up toward my hand like I knew she'd pump her body toward my cock.

My cock was on fire. I rubbed it along her ass, over and over. I was going to show her everything, and it was clear I'd come when she did.

If nothing else, I was determined to make her come.

I left her breast and added my hand to the other, sliding my finger along her slit and pushing it deep inside her.

She gasped and spread her legs further apart.

And when I pushed two fingers inside her, her keening cry rang out.

I didn't know what he was doing with my body but damn, it felt good. I should tell him to stop, but I couldn't. No, it was all I could do not to shout at him to do more.

Why hadn't my husband done this for me?

I felt betrayed, which made me feel as if I was being mean to his memory.

I brushed aside the feeling for later. Now wasn't the time to think about Sveth. All I could focus on was Madr. The way he kept rubbing his cock against my back. The way his fingers teased one special place between my legs. And the way his other fingers were pumping inside me, driving me closer to something I sensed would change my perspective forever.

I felt like I was spiraling, like something inside me kept tightening and loosening, but each time it got tighter, I was on the cusp of . . . I couldn't imagine what.

Shooting all the way to the stars. Was that even possible?

He kept rubbing. I kept pumping my hips up to meet his fingers. Everything inside me built, then slid back. Until—

With a groan, I shattered, my body shuddering and that intimate place between my legs milking Madr's fingers. He kept moving them, his thumb teasing at the top, while I rode the feeling, cresting and releasing over and over.

Finally, I collapsed on top of him, limp and completely spent.

He slid his fingers out of my body, and I braced myself for him to mock me. He'd proved his point. I *did* have a secret spot—a couple of them, actually—that gave me more pleasure than I'd ever experienced before.

But he said nothing. We continued to lazily float in the river until he turned us around and, using a scissoring of his legs, propelled us back upstream to where we'd begun. Only then did he drop his legs down to touch the bottom. He held me in his arms gently as he made his way to the edge of the river, where he lowered my feet to the ground.

He took a drying cloth and rubbed me all over.

By the time he'd finished, that place between my legs had heated up once more. I wanted to beg him to do it again, to make me fall apart like he had already, but I wasn't sure how to ask.

I wasn't sure I *should* ask. Here I'd thought I was

savvy about what went on between males and females, but I knew nothing.

He helped me dress, a silly thing for him to do. I could certainly do it myself. But I couldn't find the will to snap or tell him to back away and leave me alone. No, I enjoyed his ministrations.

I wanted more.

And that scared me more than the thought of shaydes attacking.

CHAPTER 14
MADR

My mate had fallen apart beautifully in my arms, but despite my urge to call her on it, I let it go. She appeared shocked by what happened.

I was still stunned that the male she'd professed to love hadn't given her this gift himself. And while it might be nice to act superior and tell her of course I was right, I didn't want to. She was my mate. I liked her. I'd soon love her, if prior mate bonds were anything to go by.

It felt wrong to mock her.

We returned to the clearing and ate. By the time we'd finished, the sun had risen, and the threat of shaydes attacking had waned.

"We should sleep during the day if we can," I said. "Come, lie beside me." I patted the ground on my right. The fire flickered merrily, and I'd just loaded it with wood.

"You want me to do this so you can touch me again." Her arms linked on her chest, and if a touch of fear didn't lurk in her pretty eyes, I'd challenge her about it.

"I want you to lie beside me because it's safer that way. I want to protect you, keep you from harm."

"You said your vox will sound the alarm if anything comes near."

"He will, but is it wrong of me to want to make sure you're safe?"

"You think I'll run while your guard is down."

I tilted my head, watching her face, but she gave nothing away. "Will you?"

"I can't defend myself." A sob choked her voice. "I'm no good with weapons even if I had one, and if a shayde attacked, it would kill me within seconds. I'm nothing. No one. That's what some villagers said. Without my husband, I'm not even worth what it costs to feed me."

"You're worth the world to me." I kept my voice patient. She needed understanding, not me snapping and snarling, something I ached to do with her village. They'd scorned her?

I'd show them my wrath.

I wanted to do so, that is.

But since I wanted her to like me, I'd make no progress if I showed a heavy hand with those she called her people.

"I'm worth the world to you because I can give you children." Her chin lifted.

"If the fates bless us with orclings, I'll be grateful to

them until my dying day, but I want you, Lyneth, my sweet human. *You.* Not what your body can give me."

"For all I know, I'm not fertile. I was with my husband for months, but I didn't get pregnant. And he tried." She pinched her eyes shut, and her voice weakened, her sudden fury spent. "*We* tried. It just didn't happen."

"You miss him."

"I do." She nodded fast, and her words burst out as if she needed to make sure I understood. "I thought I loved him. No, I did." Her hands flipped up. "I think I did, that is. Why can't I definitively state that? I liked him from the moment we met, and he was a good husband. That's enough, but love . . . I'm not sure I know what that is right now."

"I'm glad he treated you well."

"Please don't think you'll be able to step into his shoes."

"I have no interest in taking his place in your life or in your heart. I just hope one day, you'll come to care for me, that you'll find a place for me beside you." *And* in her heart, but how could I ask for something like that?

A touch of sadness filled me, but I shoved it away. We'd just met. How could I expect her to like, let alone love me?

"Feelings take time to grow," I said.

Her sigh whooshed out, and her body seemed to deflate along with it. "I needed you to know that."

"I understand."

"I'll lie with you. You're right; I need protection and you're big, strong, and you're good with that staff." With that, she rounded the fire and laid down on the ground between me and the fire.

I dropped next to her, moving in close to her back, though I didn't press myself against her like I wanted to.

One day, I would.

And on that day, she'd welcome my touch.

CHAPTER 15

LYNETH

Somehow, I slept through the day, waking as sunlight slaked across the forest.

I found Madr crouched nearby, feeding the fire. Brakkis stood rather than squatting on his haunches like he'd been when I fell asleep. He stretched out his wings, and I marveled at how beautiful he was, like a big golden bird.

I also marveled at how attractive Madr was, big and strong like his vox. The wind swept through the meadow, stirring his hair, making the dark strands woven through with mossy green glisten in the late-day sunlight.

I couldn't drag my eyes away from him, and was it wrong that I mentally stroked the thick muscles of his shoulders and back, that I sighed over the shape of his hips?

He appeared pensive, feeding one stick into the fire

after another, watching as the flames licked around them.

"There's food near the fire for you. Water in the flask." He didn't look my way.

"Thank you." Sitting up, I rubbed my face and grimaced at the snarls that had taken over my hair. With a sigh, I rose and went to my bag, digging around until I found a comb. I sat near Madr and struggled to get it through the mats.

"Let me do that for you, please?" he asked.

How could I snap when he asked so nicely, when he looked at me with a touch of hope in his gorgeous green eyes?

When I handed over the comb, he sat and tugged me up onto his lap facing away from him. He had thick thighs. Even my ass didn't cover the available surface.

My laugh rang out, and it was touched with a sound that told me if I wasn't careful, I'd break. I wasn't sure how I'd put the pieces of me back together again after I did.

"Why do you laugh?" he asked as he slowly worked from the bottom of my hair toward the top. He didn't tug on a snarl once, and there was something sensual about the way he did it. As if he took care because he didn't want to cause me even a slight bit of pain.

"Just thinking about how you're much bigger than me."

"I'm average sized for an orc."

"And I'm an average sized woman, but still."

"I suppose some might find it comical."

"Do you?" I didn't look back, just closed my eyes and savored how nice it felt to have someone do something kind for me. No one had since my sister joined the hunt.

Not even Sveth.

"Not really," he said. "You're the size the fates made you, as am I."

I didn't like thinking about Sveth like that. He'd loved me. He'd told me that more than once. He'd moved me into his home and made sure I had a decent kitchen to prepare our meals. He told me I didn't have to work unless I wanted to, that he made enough for us both.

Why hadn't he shown me how much pleasure could be found in the bedroom?

"Many of the women mated with my people live in the city near my home," Madr said. "When we're settled, we could visit some of them. Even my half-brother is mated with a woman. She's amazing. They have a little girl, and she's such a delight. I want to hold her and kiss her pretty cheeks all the time."

"I bet you're a wonderful uncle." I could picture him holding that little girl. "Does she look more like her mother or her father?"

"Some of both. She has her father's berry-tinged hair and his greenish-gold skin. Her features and body are more delicate like her mother's, and her eyes are bright blue."

"Like her mother or does her father have blue eyes?"

"They're like her mother's. Her name's Shirra, and I adore her."

From this, I could tell he'd be a good father, that he'd dote on his children—orclings. I suspected he'd also dote on their mother.

A strange longing shot through me, making my bones melt. I leaned back as he continued to patiently work the snarls from my hair. Closing my eyes, I completely relaxed. When was the last time I had the chance to do that? Kael took me in, but like with Sveth, I needed to cook, mend his clothing, clean the house, plus find work. Also like when I lived with my husband, there was never time to do something solely for me. And that was all right. It was a woman's role in life. Women were taught they didn't need anything but to please those around them.

Why did I now long for more?

"I don't like how my mind keeps taking me in odd directions," I said.

"In what way?"

"I was happy in the village. Happy with my husband, and I guess you could say I was content enough when Kael took me in and gave me a new home. We . . . weren't intimate, if that's what you're thinking."

"I never thought you were, though if you had been, it would make sense."

"Is it common for an orc female to go from one male to another like she's changing her clothing?" I asked, a bit of spunk coming through in my voice.

"I don't know many orc females. Most were killed when the shaydes attacked all at once. We'd placed our females who weren't skilled enough to fight in a safe location, but the shaydes found them. The blood . . ."

When he shuddered, I wanted to turn around and hug him. "Did you lose family?"

"My mother. Many friends."

An orc female he'd loved? I didn't like that jealousy stabbed through me at the thought. Madr may have claimed me, but that didn't mean I'd claimed him.

"I'm sorry," I said. "I lost my parents to the shaydes. They're nasty creatures, and I wish they'd all die."

He chuckled. "So do I. We're doing our best to make that happen."

"Do they serve a purpose?"

"I assume you mean will there be an issue if we eliminate them. I suppose they do. When they're not hunting us, they eat carcasses killed by disease or injury."

"Are there other creatures that would do this instead?"

"Perhaps."

"We can leave a few. I can't believe I'm saying that. Not when they killed my parents and so many others."

"I understand what you mean. In life, there should be balance."

"Yes, that's it. Killing them all might upset the balance. But they can stay far away from all of us. Creep into the woods at night and do their clean-up, then disappear at dawn."

"They pretty much do that right now." He set the comb aside and smoothed my hair with his fingers. Stroked it. It felt good, and I closed my eyes and leaned into his touch. "When Brakkis has healed," he said, "And he's well on his way to healing already, we'll fly at night and rest during the day. We have two nights left to travel to reach my home."

"You said it's in the mountains."

"Yes, the view of the sea is amazing from there. It was my mother's family home, and I inherited it from her. I'm grateful to have it."

I was curious enough about this male who called me his mate to wonder what his home might be like. Was it simple or fancy? Would I be happy to call it my own?

Wrong, Lyneth, I thought. As soon as I tracked down my sister's location, I would run to her and beg her to find a place for me in her life.

If only my heart didn't pinch at the thought of no longer seeing Madr.

CHAPTER 16
MADR

"You can sleep if you want," I told Lyneth later that day, as the sun slipped out of view. "I'll keep watch."

Chitters rang out in the distance.

"You think I can sleep while they hunt?" she whispered, barely audible to me, though I stood right beside her.

"You could try."

My mate had spent the day alternating between sitting beside the fire, walking around the meadow, and napping. We'd only talked about general things. What her favorite meal was. What she did in her free time—she indicated she hadn't had much free time. That made me sad. Everyone should be able to do things they enjoyed, things solely for themselves.

She'd also seemed melancholy, but that was to be

expected. She'd been ripped from the only world she'd ever known and thrust into mine.

I'd do all I could to help her adjust.

She rose to her feet and paced around the fire. "I slept during the day. I'm well rested." Stopping in front of me, she held out her hand. "Do you have a weapon I can have?"

I grabbed one of my spare knives from my pouch, laying it in her hand. "Do you know how to use it?"

"Not in the least, though I'm excellent at cutting vegetables and meat." Her head tilted, and she looked up at me with an odd expression, as if she was afraid to ask me for a favor. "Could you teach me some basic skills with this knife?"

"You're tiny."

"And mighty." The smile flashed across her face so fast, I nearly missed it.

My heart flipped over. What would it be like to have her look at me like that all the time? I prayed to the fates it would one day happen.

"You do appear strong for a human female," I said.

She snickered, another new for us. "I know we're littler than you, but we're tough inside where it counts. How else could I have survived the death of my parents and . . . well, you know?"

Clouds filled her face, and I assumed she was thinking of her lost mate again. Mourning him.

"When did he die?" I asked, needing to know.

"He died within two months of our marriage."

Since she sounded neutral, I aimed for the same tone. "I'm sorry."

"Not too much, though, am I right?" she said with a surprising laugh.

"Why would you say that? I'd never wish harm on another." Other than my cousin, I supposed. I'd like to see him come to harm for injuring Brakkis.

"Married females are not entered into the hunt. If I was still with him, I wouldn't be here with you right now.

"And that would be a true tragedy." Again, I took my cue from her, adding a bit of lightness to my voice. Her mood was softening, and that cheered me up considerably. If she could laugh with me, even tease me, she may one day love me.

Perhaps her introspection during the day had helped her resolve herself to this new life with me.

Her snort rang out and she turned away from me. "I need to go to the woods." She hefted her knife in her hand. "I'll bring this for protection."

And me. I followed right behind her.

"You don't need to come with me."

"Oh, but I do. I'm not letting you out of my sight."

"Ah. I suspect you're thinking about my secret spot." A teasing tone came through in her voice, and I couldn't stop grinning.

"Perhaps I need to show you where it is again."

"And perhaps I'll permit you to touch it once more."

I gulped and stopped just inside the woods, gaping as she continued to sashay forward. "You will?"

"I will if you'll show me where *your* secret spot is."

CHAPTER 17
LYNETH

I was dipping my toe into the fire, and if I wasn't careful, I'd be scorched.

Something had changed between us during the day, and I wasn't sure if I liked it or not. We'd talked, though not about anything significant.

I'd softened toward him when I should've maintained my guard. His touch and his smile were dangerous. If I wasn't careful, I'd . . .

No, I wouldn't fall in love with him. I *couldn't*.

I'd loved *Sveth,* and I'd never believed I'd find another who could fill my heart. I huffed out a sigh. Here I was, doubting myself again when I shouldn't.

Although, there was a lot one might consider lovable in Madr.

With my thoughts in complete disarray, I relied on moonlight to guide me into the woods, stopping in a likely spot where I listened, not hearing anything moving nearby.

Madr turned away without my asking, scanning the woods with an intent gaze that made me feel safe and secure. It was a nice feeling; one I hadn't felt in a long time.

After I finished, I walked back to the fire and added some wood, noting he'd replenished the pile. He'd also propped sticks against rocks, holding the tips over the flames. Sometime during the day, he'd also found meat.

"When did you hunt?" I asked softly.

"A reskit pretty much scrambled out into the meadow. While you were napping, I took it down from where I stooped beside the fire. It's not a lot of meat, but it'll break up the berry cakes."

"Which are tasty, but we'll get tired of them." And I'd noted we only had a few days' worth left. He'd brought more than he might need for two days' travel, which was smart. At this point, we didn't know when we'd be able to leave this area.

"I'll have Brakkis test his wing tomorrow," he said. "If he's ready, we'll fly."

"I can't imagine flying on a creature like Brakkis. I didn't even realize such a thing was possible."

"Orcs have flown with voxes for many generations. Longer than our oldest elder can remember."

The vox grazed in the meadow, but at his name, looked in our direction. True affection shone in his eyes, and it spoke well for Madr that a creature he'd raised from the time it was young liked him. I could tell Madr was a good male. Any female would be happy to have him.

"Here." Madr handed me the end of one of the sticks holding a generous amount of reskit.

"It smells wonderful."

"I seasoned it with a few herbs I found growing wild on the edge of the woods."

"My mother was an herbalist." Sitting, I dug into the reskit, sliding an almost too-hot chuck off the end with my teeth. I hissed and sucked in air as I chewed. The flavors burst on my tongue, making my belly growl.

We ate quickly, finishing every bit, and he handed me the water flask.

"Nearly empty," I said. "I'll go with you to refill it."

"We can swim while we're there if you'd like."

Nothing in his voice or on his face suggested he was thinking of anything but swimming, but my body heated.

Was it wrong of me to want him to touch me again, let alone to tease him about it?

I'd see how things went at the river.

"All right." Rising, I gathered more clothing and started in that direction, Madr joining me with his own things in hand.

We walked quietly, not wishing to draw attention.

At the river, I took time to wash the clothing I'd worn the day before. I draped the items on a big rock, planning to dry them on sticks by the fire overnight.

Madr stooped down and refilled the flask, placing it near his clean loin cloth, and started washing the one he'd worn before.

I'd never seen a male do laundry before, and if it wasn't dark and the shaydes didn't hunt, I'd chuckle. Instead, I watched him in awe. He was doing a good job; it was clear this wasn't the first time he'd washed his clothing.

Then I realized this could be my time for privacy to wash. Turning away from him, I quickly stripped and stepped into the water, moving in quickly until my chest was covered. I wasn't sure I'd ever get used to bathing in front of anyone. Even back in the village, I'd only done so when I was alone and in the dark.

No wonder some women had no knowledge of their own bodies. We were told to bathe quickly and to never let a male look upon our naked flesh in the full light of day.

Even on my wedding night, I'd stripped quickly in the dark and donned a floor-length nightie that had covered my body through the night other than during the brief time Sveth lifted it to my waist for . . .

Usually, thinking about him would bring on my sobs. Now I could only focus on the fact that he'd never touched my breasts, not once. He hadn't rolled my nipples or stroked my belly.

And when he'd kissed me, I'd felt nothing.

What would it be like to kiss Madr? He was so

sensual, I suspected it would feel amazing. *That*, I had heard other women whispering about.

I wasn't sure if I wanted to ask him to do it or not. Maybe orcs didn't kiss. Or their tusks dug into the other person's chin, and it hurt.

"Would you like me to wash your hair again?" Madr asked from close behind me.

I spun in the water, realizing I'd been slowly drifting with the current, that I'd done nothing to clean my body.

"Thank you," I said, pivoting back to give him easy access. "I can wash yours."

His low laugh rang out, so quiet, I doubted the sound reached the shore. "I'd like that, but you don't need to."

"You do it for me, and I'll do it for you."

"All right."

He gently wet my hair and lathered it, urging me to lie back on his chest like the last time while he rinsed out the suds. Then he handed me the bar.

I swam around behind him, and he submerged himself to wet his hair. He truly didn't need my help, but it felt good to do this. "Lean back," I croaked, and he lowered the back of his head onto my chest. I couldn't support his weight like he had mine, but his arms moved at his sides, keeping his body afloat.

I lathered his hair, enjoying the silky feel between my fingers. His horns jutted up from his temples and splayed a bit to the sides. They were as long as my hand, and firm, coming to a snubbed point at the tip. I assumed long ago—or even recently for that matter—orcs would use them for defense.

"That feels good," he groaned. "My horns . . ." He swallowed. "It's arousing when you touch them."

Gasping, I lifted my hands away, but he grabbed onto my arms and returned them to his horns.

"I like it," he said. "You did mention wanting to know my secret spots. This is one."

"I'm not sure that it's fair of me to arouse you," I said carefully.

"Because you're not offering me your body?"

I shrugged, then realized he couldn't see the gesture. "I've seen your cock, as you know. I still cannot imagine how it would fit inside me. Surely orcs don't push all of it within such a small space."

"I assure you, we do." Humor made his voice shake. "And I also assure you, women enjoy it."

"The place where you touched me is at the top, not inside where the cock goes."

"I have more than one cock."

"How is that possible?" I blinked for a moment. "Do you push *two* of them inside at once?" I should be horrified at the thought, but instead I tingled down there.

"No, we only push in the larger one."

Impossible. That one wouldn't fit, let alone a second. "I didn't see anything like that on your body."

"You're welcome to look closer."

"I'm sure you'd like that."

"I'd like it even more if you touched them, but that's for the future."

I wanted to say never but I couldn't. It wouldn't be true. A big part of me wanted to touch him in places other than his horns—which I was stroking. Realizing this, I paused, though I continued to rest my fingertips on them.

"My second cock is smaller than the first and above it," he said.

I almost called him on this, asked him to show me, prove it, but I wasn't sure I wanted to take this in that direction.

"My second cock is made for your secret spot."

My fingers stilled on his horns, and I noted I'd started stroking them again, running my fingertips up and down the lengths. I could almost imagine they were his cock, that I was touching his very fire.

In the deepest part of my soul, I wanted to touch his cock in the same way.

I dragged my fingers off his horns and finished rinsing his hair. "I'm not sure I understand." For an experienced woman, I felt woefully unprepared for this conversation.

"The smaller cock attaches itself to that small nub at the top of your opening, called a clit, and it sucks."

My breath caught at the thought. Swallowing hard, I struggled to ignore that my thighs ached. I wanted to spread them wide and tell Madr to show me what his second cock could do.

Madr dropped his feet into the water and turned to face me, moving so close I could feel his cock pressing against my thigh. While his feet held our position, he placed one arm around me to keep my head above water. Taking my other hand, he guided it to his groin.

I should snatch my hand away, but I was greedy for this knowledge—so I told myself.

Actually, I was quickly becoming greedy for Madr.

CHAPTER 18
MADR

I watched Lyneth's face as I guided her hand to my cocks, ready to ease away from her if she showed any resistance.

My seductive game was seducing me as easily as her.

"I have a main cock, as you've noted," I said with a grin. She was with me so far, and that made my heart sing. "Would you like to touch that first?"

She jerked her gaze up to mine, and I read confusion and a touch of wonder in her eyes. "Why would anyone touch it?"

"Because it feels good when it's touched, like your clit."

"I suspect I have more than one secret spot," she said shyly.

"You mean your opening."

"Where a cock goes."

My pulse surged. For a woman who'd been mated,

Lyneth came across completely innocent. I couldn't imagine what her mate had done with her in bed, though I'd begun to suspect he focused solely on his own needs and not once considered hers.

"Yes, that place." My voice came out guttural with anticipation. "There are other places inside the opening that will bring you pleasure. A cock strokes them as it moves inside you."

"Why didn't I feel that?" she growled. "I didn't, and his cock moved inside me."

I didn't like speaking about the dead, but at this point, I wanted to slice him to pieces. I wanted to tell her that her mate hadn't done his duty as her husband. But she'd loved him, and I'd never try to step into the middle of that. There was a place for me with her, and I'd find my way to it.

"I believe it helps if a woman is first aroused. Your body will then make things wet. Slick." Damn, my cock ached. Talking about this was arousing me even further. "Once a woman is wet inside, the cock will move easily. And I promise you . . ." I chuckled to lighten the mood. "My cock will not only fit inside you, but you'll also enjoy it when it's there."

She shook her head slowly, frowning, and extended her hand toward me.

I placed it on the head of my cock, and my shaft jerked up toward her.

A hint of a smile flirted across her mouth. "It's vigorous."

As was I. It was all I could do not to laugh, but I sensed she'd back away immediately if I did.

"You can touch it, stroke it like you did my horns. That feels good."

"As good as when you rubbed my . . . clit?" She darted a look up at my face before ducking her own.

She was so sweet. So perfect.

"Yes, just as good," I said.

Her hand tightened, and she moved it up and down, squeezing. If I didn't know better, I'd think she'd done this before.

"Above my other cock, between where it's now positioned and my abdomen, is my second cock. Some call it a spur."

"Can I touch that too?"

"I'd love it if you did."

She gave me a look full of power, as if she already realized what her simple touch did to me. Leaving my cock, she trailed her fingers down my abs, making me twitch because it tickled. When she wrapped her hand around my spur, my groan ripped out.

Sucking in a deep breath, she met my gaze. "It feels good to be in control of this."

"There's a way we could be intimate, that you could test my cock, so to speak, while still being in control."

Her head tilted. "How?"

"I'll lie on my back, and you can sit above me."

"I can't even imagine how—" Her frown deepened

before her face cleared. "Oh, you're suggesting I sit on you and guide your cock inside me."

"When you're ready, of course. Never before then."

"I don't know yet if I'm ready."

"You tell me. I'm at your disposal."

"Hmm." She continued to squeeze and rub my spur, and my main cock bobbed against her hand, stealing some of the strokes. "I haven't found anything on your spur that suggests it can suck."

"You'd have to be in the right position. It'll attach to your clit and stretch as I move inside you."

"Or as I move over you."

When had my mate become so bold? "Yes, then as well."

"I'll think about this."

"Of course. There's no rush." It was going to kill me to wait. Talking about this was almost as arousing as touching her. Which . . .

"While you're exploring my cock, would you like me to show you the spot inside you that feels pleasure, the one my cock will stroke when I'm pumping deeply within you?"

Her lips twisted, though I could tell she wasn't irritated about my boldness by the twinkle in her eyes. "Yes, I believe you should show me. I don't like not knowing these things about my body."

I scooped her up and carried her to the shore, laying her on a flat rock. After peering around and listening, determining we were still alone, I leaned over her. "We haven't kissed."

Her lips curled up. "Are you suggesting I have a special spot in my mouth?"

"Perhaps."

"Then *perhaps* you should kiss me, and we can find out."

CHAPTER 19

LYNETH

I wasn't sure why I trusted him to show me all the secret spots on my body, but for some reason, I did.

And when he claimed my mouth with his own, I forgot about everything but him.

His kiss mesmerized me, drew me in, and I suspected I'd cling to him until he decided to stop.

I also wasn't sure I liked how he knew all this, but it was time I discovered exactly what my body could do.

As his mouth moved on mine, I cupped his shoulders and pulled him down fully on top of me, savoring the feel of his weight. He was so much bigger than me, yet he didn't crush me since he supported his lower body with his knees.

When his knee slid higher between my legs, and he rubbed my clit, I gasped. His tongue dipped into my mouth, seeking mine.

As his lips molded perfectly against my mouth, I could taste a subtle hint of mint. The softness and warmth of his mouth ignited a tingling sensation inside me that spread through every bit of my body. His tongue gently danced with mine, making me feel things I'd never dreamed were possible.

A woman's desire. A need I couldn't define, though it centered between my legs.

And the beginning of caring.

Danger lay in that direction, but I couldn't seem to help it. I wanted Madr if only for this moment.

Our kiss was more than just the taste, though. With every flick of his tongue, he made electricity course through me, like a bolt of lightning connecting us on a deeper level. He was a heady intoxication, and I sensed I was going to crave his touch for a lifetime.

In no time, I was lost in the sensation, the melding of our lips, the way they moved together in perfect harmony.

This first kiss was more than an act of physical intimacy. It was a gateway to a world of wonder and exploration, a journey he was gently and carefully leading me on. He was giving me a glimpse into the limitless possibilities that awaited me if I chose to remain with him. There was nothing I could do but surrender to the intensity of the moment.

He lifted his head. "Mate," he growled, his voice full of possession. He gave me a quick smile before kissing down to my breast.

While he sucked my nipple into his hot mouth, his knee shifted to the side. I barked out a cry of joy at the feel of his tongue on my breast but whimpered that he took his knee away.

His fingers roamed across my belly, moving between my legs, and I had no shame. I parted my thighs, welcoming him to do whatever he pleased.

No, to do what he knew would please me.

I was overwhelmed by the sensations that raced through me as he continued to explore my body. Every touch, every caress, made me buck up against him. He'd turned me into a greedy woman, and I loved it. Thrived on it. His hands, warm and rough yet gentle, traced along the curves of my body, mapping out every spot that only he seemed to know.

His fingers found their way between my legs, and I gasped at the contact. They moved with a grace and precision that left me breathless, teasing and stroking. Wetness filled that space between my thighs, evidence that I ached for his touch.

As he continued to stroke my clit, I jerked my hips up, aching to feel his fingers deep within me once more. I was acutely aware of his every movement. The soft brush of his lips on my breast and the scratchy feel of his tongue on my nipple. I had a sensitive spot there too, and as he sucked, sparks shot through me, centering between my legs. With each stroke, he awakened new feelings within me, feelings I never knew were possible.

I closed my eyes to immerse myself in the moment,

focusing on the multitude of feelings overwhelming my senses. The scent of his skin mixed with the heady aroma of my desire. I should be embarrassed by the wet sounds my body made in response to his touch, the whimpers that erupted from my throat, and the growls he released to show me how much he enjoyed my response.

He slid his fingers inside me and twisted them, pressing on one particular spot that made fire roar through me. I released a guttural groan, and he left my breast only long enough to shoot me a smile. "That's it, correct?"

I could only nod. I braced my heels on the rock and started pumping my hips up hard against his hand. I'd lost all control, and I wanted one thing: the satisfaction he'd given me the day before.

He sucked on my breast, running his tongue across the nipple over and over while one hand pumped deeply within me, stroking that one certain area with each pass. His thumb remained on my clit, rubbing, and I could only imagine how amazing it might be if something latched onto it and sucked.

The feeling grew inside me too fast, pulling me along with it.

It burst free, and I cried out as my body shuddered. I was consumed by the feeling.

Consumed by Madr.

While my body slowly returned and my brain remembered how to focus, he continued to move his fingers gently inside me. Each stroke made ripples of pleasure float across my bones.

Finally, he removed his fingers from my body and carefully licked them. "You taste amazing mate. One day soon, I'm going to need more."

At this point, he could take it, and I wouldn't protest.

As we rose, rinsed in the water, and he dried my body with a cloth, it was hard to admit he had such a profound effect on me. My bones were humming, and my clit still throbbed. To think I hadn't even known that small pearl down there existed.

Even after I dried between my legs, it still felt wet down there—the moisture he'd spoken of. He'd made my body produce it with his touch.

I may be innocent and naïve, but even I could tell I was still vaguely aroused. The true definition of that term was new to me. In my mind, arousal was solely for males, never a female.

What a disservice women did to each other when we didn't speak of this from the time a woman was old enough to wed. Instead of discussing clits and inner secret spots, let alone wetness, someone whispered to me that it was my place as a wife to go to my husband's bed and lie with him. That he'd show me what happened after that. That my role was solely to please him.

No one said I should find pleasure myself.

Bitterness filled my mouth at the realization that my husband probably hadn't known anything more about my body than me. I couldn't remain angry with him, however, and not because I'd loved him. We were both a product of the world we grew up in, and perhaps males didn't discuss secret spots any more than females. It wasn't as if we were born with this knowledge.

"Where did you learn how to please a female?" I asked when we'd dressed and quietly returned to the meadow. At least we hadn't encountered shaydes yet, though I suspected we were on borrowed time.

"Males are taught such things when we're old enough to understand," he said. He took my wet clothing from me and draped it over tree branches to dry.

After feeding the fire, he sat near it and tugged me down onto his lap, facing him.

"I don't believe males in my village are taught anything," I said with irritation painting my voice.

He shrugged. "Some species don't believe in sharing that sort of information. Fortunately for me—and you," His grin rose, and he was too damn appealing when he smiled, "Fortunately for us both, orcs are taught about such things. Of course, we titter among ourselves in between lessons, but we listen raptly when the older males explain about clits and spots on a female that bring pleasure."

"You have formal instructions?" I couldn't quite believe this.

"Nothing like that. It's more like this moment, a loose gathering of males who go hunting and on their way back home, they stop for a time and sit around a fire."

"Discussing clits?" I scoffed.

"How else will we know how to find them, let alone what to do with them?"

"And you were how old when they discussed this?"

"Fifteen."

I sighed. "That's much too young to be talking about clits and giving females pleasure."

He shrugged. "That's how it's done with orcs." His grin rose, and I realized he'd been rubbing my back, his big hands moving all the way down my ass with each stroke. It felt good. Few other than my now-dead parents and older sister had touched me. Closing my eyes, I leaned back into his hands, savoring how strong he was, yet gentle. I sensed he'd never do anything that might hurt me. That if he did, he'd be horrified, not dismiss it as me being too sensitive or soft.

To my surprise, he eased me off his lap and rose. "Let me check on Brakkis and make sure we're completely alone. I also want to make a soft place for you on the ground."

I nodded, my body feeling dreamy and relaxed. "Can I help?" Assuming I could host enough energy to get up off the ground.

"I want to do this for you, sweet one."

"Then I'll just sit here. Stare into the fire."

He started walking away but turned back. "What would you think about me using my mouth in addition to my fingers to show you pleasure the next time?"

Funny how he assumed there would be a next time.

But I couldn't voice a complaint or tell him he could no longer touch me. If he curled his finger, I suspected I'd rise and strip off my clothing then walk toward him with complete abandonment.

"Use your mouth in what way?" I frowned, but more from confusion than reluctance.

"It could be a surprise."

"Like my clit?"

"Your clit will enjoy my tongue."

Heat seared across my skin, and I fanned my face. I should tell him no, correct? "Surely that's much too decadent a thing for you to do." Mouths down there? I couldn't imagine.

Actually, I could. His mouth would be wet, warm, and his tongue . . .

"I'll enjoy it." His smile widened. "And so will you."

CHAPTER 20

MADR

I carefully checked Brakkis's wing, pleased to see the webbing had sealed over and that it didn't seem to hurt him when I moved it. I gave him a complete rubdown because he loved it, then kissed his snout.

While he settled on the grass, his gaze scanning the area, I entered the woods and climbed as high in a tree as I dared. Listening, I waited for any sound that might indicate shaydes approached. They were bold, but they feared voxes and fire. We'd burned their breeding grounds when we sought vengeance for them killing so many of our females.

While up in the tree, I contemplated bringing Lyneth up here to sleep in my arms, but I felt confident Brakkis would snort if anything came close to the meadow.

Back on the ground, I gathered soft needle branches and brought the big cluster to the smooth area near the fire. After collecting enough wood for the night, I spread the branches out to make a bed.

Then I used some of our water to wash my hands.

Lyneth watched me throughout, her eyes gleaming with a look I couldn't define. She was softening, and that thrilled me.

Would she ever love me? Just as she was fated to be my mate, so too was I fated to love her. It would suck if she didn't feel the same. However, that had never happened with true mates, and I needed to trust she'd find her way to me.

I needed to stop thinking about what might or might not happen in the future and focus on now.

For someone trying to seduce his mate, I wasn't doing a very good job with it. When I was stroking her delectable ass, why hadn't I laid her down by the fire and continued what I'd begun by the river? I sensed she would've let me do whatever I pleased.

Instead, I'd nudged her away, patted my vox, collected branches, and made sure we were safe.

That was why.

I'd put everything off because protecting my precious mate and making sure Brakkis was comfortable mattered a lot to me. It would be wrong for me to let everything go and give her more pleasure if I hadn't first ensured we could be together without worrying about something attacking us.

"Come sit with me by the fire?" I asked.

She glanced at the nest I'd made. "Are you sure you don't wish for me to lie down?"

I loved the teasing tone in her voice.

"Oh, I do wish for you to lie down," I said. "Very much so."

The smile that lifted on her face was both sensual and sweet. "Perhaps I should remove my clothing before I sit in your lap?"

My groan ripped out of me. Was *I* seducing her or was it the other way around?

Her smile wavered. "I'm making you uncomfortable."

"You're making me long for you. So much."

She dropped down beside me and stared into the flames. "I don't understand much of this, as you can tell. I know I should, but back in the village, women aren't taught about their bodies or those of males, not like orcs. Are your females shown how to find their special spots?"

"I assume so. I never asked."

"But they're sophisticated about their bodies. They know what can give them great pleasure and they know how to seek it."

"You're correct."

"My village does us a grave disservice."

I laughed, enjoying this conversation with her despite my wish to lick her clit and give her another orgasm. "Each culture handles things like this in a different way. When—all right, *if*—we have orclings, we'll raise them with other orcs. We'll teach them all they need to know, not only about their own bodies but the world around them. This I promise you."

Her gaze darted away from mine to her hands on her lap. "What if I don't want to stay with you?"

"After the orgasm I gave you yesterday?" I grunted before she could speak. "I tease. And I'll admit, I've thought of this as well. As I flew here on Brakkis, I didn't know if the fates would match me with someone and if they did, whether she'd wish to remain with me or I with her. Would the fates randomly connect people who can't get along? I doubt this. How could they? But I also told myself I wouldn't cling even if I fell in love." I tipped her head up to meet her eyes. "But it's easier to say such a thing when I was thinking of a possible mate. It's much harder to think of this with you."

"You can't love me."

I read two meanings in her words and addressed the first because I wasn't sure I wanted to analyze what she might mean if she was saying I *shouldn't* love her. Everyone deserved love. "I believe I *could* love you, and that's what matters."

Actually, I was at least halfway there, but that was common with mate bonds. The couple fell for each other quickly.

"You barely know me," she said.

"We've been together two days with no one here but us. I've seen how you handle something new, how you've remained strong when you must've assumed something horrible would happen to you, and how you aren't afraid of my vox."

She scoffed. "He's like an overgrown chall."

"He'll purr like a chall if you stroke his cheeks."

She frowned Brakkis's way. "Really?"

"Close enough. And here's the thing."

She tilted her head to the side to watch my face.

"If you stroke me, I suspect you'll find I also purr."

LYNETH

Back at the river, I felt wild. Free. Now I felt like running away, and I knew why. Madr was stepping into the sad, lonely place inside me I swore no one else would ever fill.

I was falling in love with him and while I should feel horrible guilt, I couldn't seem to drum up the emotion. I could tell myself Sveth wouldn't want me to mourn him forever, and I was sure that would be true, but that felt too much like me making an excuse to let myself give in to Madr's lure.

"You should sleep," he said softly. Did he suspect how my emotions were churning, how unsettled I felt about him?

He knew my body better than I did myself. I bet he understood my feelings just as well. I wasn't sure what to think about that.

"I'm not used to any of this," I said, my voice creaking with pain.

"Take the time you need, mate. Always." He patted the soft pine needle bed he'd made for me. Even in this, he understood my needs and catered to them as if they were more important than his own.

I dropped down onto the bed, huffing like a petulant child. "I just don't know what to do!"

I felt as if I struggled to hold onto something, though I didn't know exactly what it might be.

My sanity? No. And it wasn't my sense of self-worth.

Oh, I knew. I worried I'd fall for Madr and get lost completely in him.

And then he'd die like Sveth.

What a silly notion. Life was death. We all knew that from the day we were born, and we had no more control over when it would rush in to claim us than we did with the weather.

He sat a moment as if contemplating my words, thinking of what he wanted to say. Even in this, he irked me. He was much too thoughtful, too kind. It made it very hard to resist him.

"It's good that you don't need to decide right now," he said. "You have lots of time before you need to figure out what you want or need. And if you still don't know your heart in a week or a month, know I'll give you more time."

"It's not fair to you." What was most unfair was my thought of leaving him.

"Is anything ever fair?" He shook his head slowly. "My answer to that is no. But all we can do is hope that the fates give us their best." He huffed a soft laugh. "And be thankful for what little they end up actually giving us." His gaze met mine. "That's you, Lyneth, whether you like it or not. But I'm not a male who will make anyone do something to please me. Know this."

I swallowed, pondering his words, and some of the anxious feeling spiraling inside me loosened.

"We'll travel a short distance in the morning to test Brakkis's wing," he said, his voice lighter. "After that, we'll find a place where we're safe enough to let him rest for the afternoon. At dark, if he does well for the first short distance, we'll travel for as much of the night as he'll allow before he needs to stop once more. Within two to three nights' travel, we'll reach my home. After that, can you give yourself the time and patience you need before you come to any big decisions?"

Did he suspect I'd try to leave him? He must. This would be the most prominent thought in each woman's mind, to escape something they feared above almost everything else: to be rutted by an orc.

Little did they know how amazing it might be to be touched by their orc mate.

"Did all the prior mate hunt women succumb to their mates quickly?" I asked.

"Not quickly." His smile was handsome. It made my heart flop around, and my skin flash with heat. One word, and I'd spread my legs for him again, and this time, I'd beg him to show me how wonderful a cock was supposed to feel sinking inside a woman. "As I said, my half-brother's mated with a woman, and they fought from the time they met."

I frowned. "Do they still fight?"

"Only for fun." He chuckled. "They adore each other. They have a love everyone should strive for. Honestly, I envy them."

"You don't want her for yourself, do you?" And there was that jealousy again, gnawing away at my toes, telling me this glorious male would never truly want someone like me.

"Not in the least. She's wonderful. I love her like a sister. I suppose I envy how happy they are. Doesn't everyone want to feel that way with their life partner?" He nodded slowly, staring into the fire, before turning my way again. "And you already know how I feel about my niece. She's the sweetest little thing. I hope they have ten just like her."

"Your brother's mate might feel differently about that."

The skin around his eyes creased with humor and affection as he thought of his brother and his family. "She did say they're taking this one orcling at a time. I'm friendly with another mated couple. Odik is caedos, leader of the Zephyr Clan. He and his mate live on an island some distance away from the shore. They love that life, and I've visited a few times. Eleri's an amazing seamstress. She sells some of her clothing in the city."

"I remember Eleri." Though only vaguely. "She was accused of a crime, but few believed she did it. The woman who accused her was always mean to Eleri, who had a limp. That came from a childhood injury, I think."

"Yes. She mentioned that. She and Odik have a sturdy son and a new daughter. She and my brother's mate talk about their children growing up together."

"You make this sound wonderful." And much less scary.

"That's me." He flashed a smile. "I only want you to feel happy, Lyneth. Know this."

"What if that means you must take me back to the village?"

"Would they welcome you back?"

I sighed. "No. I'm a gift to the orcs in exchange for protection from the shaydes. They'd never risk the treaty for one such as me."

"You're worth risking any treaty."

My heart surged at the huskiness in his voice.

"You don't believe the fates chose you for me?" he asked.

I was beginning to suspect they might've.

But admitting that would mean releasing everything I still clung to inside me.

CHAPTER 22
MADR

T was dozing beside my mate when I heard a subtle sound in the woods.

Shayde.

With my pulse thrumming in my throat, pounding so loudly it nearly deafened me, I left her side, grateful she still slumbered and wasn't awake and afraid. I had enough fear for us both.

I'd battled shaydes. Dresalods too, now that I no longer heeded my father's demands to remain hidden when they attacked.

But each time I fought a beast in the past, I could focus solely on defeating it. Now I had a precious mate to protect.

When the creature crept into the meadow as far from Brakkis as it could, my vox grunted and rose to his feet. He raked his claws across the ground, digging deep furrows.

He hissed and stomped toward the shayde, stopping when I held up my hand. We trained our voxes to obey both foot and hand commands from the time they slipped form the seed, and I was never more grateful I'd remained patient with Brakkis until he learned them all, because now he obeyed me without question.

A nudge of my head, and a wave toward the fire and Lyneth told him what I needed.

Protect my mate.

He bowed his head and moved toward her, hovering near her.

With my flail lifted, I raced toward the shayde.

It galloped toward me, its claws digging into the ground.

I leaped before we slammed into each other and smacked onto its spine, driving my staff down on its head. It reared up and twisted, throwing me off. I landed hard in the grass but rolled with my staff tucked in close, rising onto my feet in a crouch.

It stared toward Lyneth, salivating.

Never my mate.

I slammed toward it, swinging my flail, and it cracked against the creature's snout. It grunted and reeled toward me, but I followed the first blow with another, this time, bringing it down hard on its neck.

With a whimper, the beast pivoted on its haunches and fled back into the woods. That wasn't enough for me. I chased it until it had outdistanced me and kept going. A quick walk around the meadow showed no others lurked, ready to attack, but I climbed a tree and listened, peering in every direction, not returning to the ground until I was sure we were alone.

"Good. Don't think of coming near our camp," I hissed, as if shaydes could hear. Perhaps they could. No one ever doubted how smart they were.

When I returned to the meadow, I found Brakkis hovering over Lyneth, who still slept. He backed away and nodded.

"You're the best," I said softly, stroking his cheeks. I gave him a rubdown and checked his wing, grateful to find it still healing, then covered the wound with more salve. Voxes healed much faster than orcs, especially their wings. Survival of those who could outlast the others, I supposed. Those in his past whose bodies healed quickly lived to produce young. Through time, the trait solidified in the species.

I fed the fire, building it larger than I probably needed to, but it was a wonderful deterrent. Shaydes may come close to investigate, but few would step out into the meadow when they saw me on alert and Brakkis standing guard.

I woke Lyneth at dawn, and we ate quickly, then packed up our camp. I put out the fire as she went over to Brakkis.

Pausing, she peered back at me. "You're sure he won't eat me?" The smile she added told me she was remembering my words about me eating her, something I couldn't wait to do when we next stopped to rest.

With a low chuckle to show me she was joking; she went around to Brakkis's face and cupped his cheeks like she must've seen me do. Leaning close, she whispered something to him I couldn't hear, and he playfully nudged her belly. After giving his brow a kiss, she sauntered over to me where I stood staring at her, my food pouch loose in my hand.

"Would you like a kiss too?" she asked sweetly.

"If you're giving them out."

"I believe I can be persuaded to give one to you."

The pouch smacked on the ground, and I lifted her up to eye level.

She held my shoulders and grinned. "I believe you *would* like a kiss."

I loved how she welcomed my touch.

Our mouths met, and she shocked me when her tongue stroked my lips, demanding entry, which I gave her.

I groaned and it was all I could do not to lay her on the ground and follow.

When she lifted her head, she grinned. "Now that was a nice kiss."

That's when I knew I was in love with Lyneth.

CHAPTER 23
LYNETH

"I've never ridden a vox before," I said as we approached Brakkis.

My mind still spun from Madr's kiss, and I couldn't wait for us to stop later. That's when I planned to ask him to show me everything his mouth could do.

Where had this needy female come from? I suspected she'd always been inside me; she just needed the right person to draw her out.

To think I left the village believing I had nothing to live for. Now it seemed as if life had given me a great gift, one I'd be foolish to refuse.

Where did that leave me with my plan to run away and find my sister? Well, if I chose to stay with Madr, maybe he'd help me find her. Then I could have both, right?

Excitement bubbled inside me at the thought. I couldn't wait to see what life had in store for me next.

Madr tossed me up onto Brakkis's back. After making sure his staff was secure in the sheath on his spine, he leaped up behind me, settling me snugly against his front. "I direct him with foot commands but be alert at all times. If he needs to, say, avoid a flock of birds or even another vox, he's been known to suddenly dive or dart to the side."

"Can I hold onto the spikes?" They jutted up his neck in front of me and looked more flexible than sharp.

"That and I'll hold onto you." His arm went around me, and I welcomed his warmth. The air wasn't particularly cool, but I imagined it would be while traveling with the wind and elevation. Although . . . "How high in the sky will he fly?"

"Some distance above the tree line. If he flies too close, he's apt to frighten birds and they swarm around him. We've even been attacked by some who were protecting their nests. As you might know, there are large birds nesting in the forest."

"I didn't go into the woods except during the day and only rarely. My sister enjoyed exploring more than me." She was an herbalist, and our village missed her healing skills. Our mayor drove her away; I knew it. Kael told me I had originally been chosen for the hunt, that the mayor picked me to hurt my sister, but that she'd taken my place. I could never repay her for what she'd done. "Did you attend the hunt last year?"

"I did."

Ah, so perhaps his clan fates would've chosen me for

him, then. I would've been angry and very sad to leave Sveth for another, but would I have finally come to accept I belonged with Madr?

It frightened me to realize how much I was coming to care for him already. It had only been a few days, but I felt as if I'd known him longer. Even worse, I suspected if I lost Madr, it would hurt a lot more than it had with Sveth. I felt disloyal for the thought, but I couldn't seem to control my emotions. They'd grabbed onto me and taken me for a wild ride. All I could do was hold on and hope I landed safely.

"Here we go," Madr said softly.

He shifted his legs, and Brakkis sprung up into the air, his wings snapping out. I had to look hard to find the spot where he'd been wounded since it was smooth and nearly healed.

We soared above the forest and kept going. Would we rise high enough to touch the clouds?

"This is amazing," I said, my heart lighter than it had been for a very long time. "It feels magical. Wonderful."

"I want to say you get used to it, but you never do."

"Could I bond with a vox sometime?"

"Perhaps. No human has gone to the breeding grounds so far. We don't know if the voxes would bond with a human, though it's certainly worth trying."

He guided Brakkis a bit higher before another nudge of his heels made the vox level out. His enormous wings swooped back and forth. I'd seen birds flying near the village, particularly over the river while hunting for fixh.

I'd even watched them for a time, marveling at how they could control their position in the sky without seeming as if they used much effort.

"He's doing well," Madr said. "He doesn't appear to be in any pain." The sorrow in his voice echoed inside me. "I want to kill my cousin for what he did."

"I'll help," I said fiercely.

He chuckled, but it faded fast. "I don't believe I'll be allowed to kill him, however, even if I explained what he did to Brakkis."

"He didn't just harm your vox, he injured him to keep him from flying, leaving you both abandoned in a forest full of shaydes."

"Yes," he sighed.

"There must be some sort of punishment for what many would consider attempted murder. Could you go to the authorities and explain? They might take care of this for you."

"Perhaps. The elders would be displeased."

"It's unfortunate that we can't attack him and do it ourselves."

His arm tightened around my waist. "I love how vicious you are, mate."

"I defend those I care for, and while I haven't known Brakkis long, he's special. Besides, he's a creature much like a pet. It's our role in life to protect those who can't do so for themselves. Brakkis has long sharp teeth and claws that could sever my head with one bite or blow, but he doesn't come across to me as a creature who'd randomly attack others."

"Voxes are generally peaceful creatures. They do fight among themselves, and they can be brutal in battle."

"How hard would it be for them to kill a shayde or a . . . I can't remember the other creature you named."

"A dresalod. They're ocean creatures who emerge and attack us, though we've recently discovered a way to kill them before we have to engage them in battle."

"How?" I pictured some kind of weapon that could be used from a distance.

"We've found that a certain plant burns them, so we've planted long rows of them along the shore. Now when the dresalods leave the water to attack, they're killed by the plant."

"That's amazing."

"It truly is. A woman discovered this, and she'd saved us all. The dresalods were attacking more and more often. We were losing voxes and orcs to them with each battle. Now most are killed before they reach the wall encircling the city."

"A human woman?"

"Yes. My brother, Jaus's mate, Rhoslyn."

CHAPTER 24

MADR

"Rhoslyn, you say?" Lyneth's voice came out high-pitched, and I couldn't tell if it was from excitement or anxiety.

"Do you remember her? She was in last year's hunt."

"I do. She's . . ." Lyneth sucked in a breath and released it. "Rhoslyn was a well-respected healer in the village."

"Yes, that's the one. She's amazing." I was gushing, but I admired my sister-in-law so much. "She discovered that lindenmint was toxic to the dresalods, and now we finally have a way to keep them from making headway when they attack. She was injured badly by a dresalod not long after she arrived in the city with my brother."

Lyneth's breath caught. "She was? She's all right now?"

"Yes. Perfectly fine. As I said, she and my brother have a new daughter, Shirra. I adore her and honestly, I want to be with her all the time. My niece is curious and happy, and there can't be a prettier or smarter orcling in the kingdom."

"She sounds special."

"She is. I'll introduce you to them when we reach the orc kingdom."

"Do you . . . live near your brother and Rhoslyn?"

"Their summer home in the mountains is close to mine. During the winter months, they live in their home in the city. Brakkis can land on their balcony, much like Jaus's vox does. Right now, though, I assume they're at Jaus's mother's estate in the mountains. They're not far away, which is good because I need to see Shirra daily." I didn't need to do more than think about my niece to feel happy.

"Could I walk to their home?"

"Oh, yes, in ten or fifteen minutes."

"So close," she breathed.

When she relaxed against my chest, I realized her posture had tightened.

"Do you remember Rhoslyn?" I asked carefully, leaning a bit to the side to see as much of her face as I could. Was she nervous about flying? She must be. I relaxed back into my position behind her.

"Rhoslyn is . . . special."

"That she is. As is my brother. Half-brother, technically, and I love him. It doesn't matter to me if we had different mothers."

"How did that come about?"

I guided Brakkis to the right to avoid a big flock of cheerish birds, and he flew easily in that direction, showing no sign he'd been injured. "My father's not a very good person."

"I'm sorry. That must've made it tough while growing up with him. I assume you lived with him?"

"I did. My father was with Jaus's mother before mine. He set her aside when he met my mother, who was his true mate."

"Ah, so orcs do this just like males in the village. We call it divorce there. It's not that common, however."

"In my father's case, he and Jaus's mother weren't mated. He set her aside and mated with my mother. While my father has ignored him, he lived close by with his mother. We trained together, wrestled, and were friends while growing up. His mother insisted on this; she was an amazing person."

"Jaus doesn't resent that you were raised by your father but he wasn't?"

"I'm sure he does, though he hasn't transferred that emotion to me. We're friends and brothers, and how that came about doesn't matter to either of us."

"You're fortunate, then."

"You've mentioned a sister. Are you two close?" I assumed her sister was back at the village, worried about Lyneth. "I could take you to her for a visit if you'd like. Jaus and Rhoslyn visited her sister, though she said they weren't allowed to speak for long."

"That's too bad."

"Yes. Rhoslyn misses her sister a lot. When she was forced from the village, she mourned her. Her sister is married. Perhaps you know her too?"

"The village has many people, but I'm sure I do. Do you . . . know her name?"

I paused, frowning, before shrugging. "If Rhoslyn mentioned it, I don't remember."

Her body softened again. Why did she keep tensing?

It must be the flying. "We're perfectly safe on Brakkis." I tightened my arm around her. "I'm so used to flying, I could probably do so in my sleep and not fall. I'll keep you safe."

She leaned back against me. "Thank you."

"As for Rhoslyn, I'm sure you encountered her healing skills even if you didn't know her well. She's becoming well known in the orc city already, and I'm sure it was the same in your village."

"There are a few healers, but I do remember one who was better than the others." She waved to the woods beneath us. "How far does this stretch?"

"All the way to the mountains. My home is on the city-side of the mountain range, and while we have trees there, they don't grow as densely as here."

"Does your home have many rooms? My parents had a nice home, but after they were killed by the shaydes, my sister and I had to move to a place where we shared one large room with a kitchen and living area. We couldn't afford anything else on my sister's wages."

"My home has many rooms." Should I tell her who I

used to be? I wasn't sure how she'd take that information. I was no longer a prince, so everything I could've claimed months ago would never be mine. My cousin would take it all unless I could convince my father to acknowledge Jaus. The thought of Riank ruling was bitter on my tongue.

"I can't imagine what it's like to live in a home with many rooms." She still sounded subdued, though she'd eventually see she had nothing to fear from flying.

Seeing that the flap of Brakkis's wings was slowing, I started looking for a good place to land.

"Orcs live in the forest too," I said. "The Matis Clan. Or Shadow Clan as we sometimes like to call it."

"Why Shadow?"

"Because you won't see them until they've placed a knife at your throat."

A shiver went through her, and I pulled her snug against my chest.

"Cold?" I asked.

She shook her head. "Just overwhelmed, I guess. I knew orcs protected the village from shaydes, but I assumed you all lived nearby."

"We rotate, each clan providing warriors for a month or more before cycling others through." I pointed to the shift of leaves across the tops of a series of trees, tracing the pattern as something moved subtly below. "See? There's a Matis Clan member now. They know we're flying above them."

"Will they attack us?" she asked in a hollow voice.

"Not a fellow orc on a vox. They're mostly friendly."

"I'm not an orc."

I tightened my arm around her. "You're with me. And no orc would ever harm a woman. You're too highly valued."

"For birthing orclings."

"That is the result, yes. But we treasure our mates; adore them, actually. None of the relationships are forced. While a rare orc would take a woman against her will, the vast majority of us wouldn't. We all seek our true mate, and we're willing to abstain until that time comes."

"And what if you never find her?"

"We can mate outside a true mating like my father did with Jaus's mother. She loved him, and I believe he cared for her at one time. He must've."

"Do orcs in the Matis Clan fly with voxes too?"

"They move quickly through the treetops, so I don't believe they've ever felt the need. None have gone to the Ember Clan's lands. The Ember Clan lives close to the vox breeding grounds. Matis Clan members don't travel like we do from the sea to distant islands or from the city to your village."

"Wow. They live high in the trees?"

"Some do. Others seem to melt into the ground. They keep that part of their lives secret, and we respect that."

"Hmm."

I guided Brakkis down toward a break in the trees ahead, and he landed lightly in a small open area made up of tall grass peppered with a few spindly trees. After slipping off him, I lifted Lyneth to the ground, holding her until I was sure she'd secured her footing.

Moving to her side, I reached up to tug our pouch of food from Brakkis's spike.

Lyneth's gasp rang out.

In one movement, I pulled my flail from its sheath and leaped, putting myself between him and whatever had startled my mate.

A line of Matis Clan warriors stood not far away with grim expressions on their faces.

Bellowing out a challenge, one of them jumped toward me, his short sword lifted.

CHAPTER 25
LYNETH

I was upset with myself for not telling Madr right away. Rhoslyn was mated to Madr's brother! I couldn't believe the coincidence. To think I was hoping to escape whoever claimed me in the hunt and find my way to my sister to beg sanctuary. Instead, she lived nearby, and she was not only related by mating to Madr, but we'd also be visiting her.

I wasn't sure why I didn't tell him immediately. The longer I held it inside, the harder the shell around my secret became, until it was nearly impossible to break through it to speak the words.

There was a big difference between deciding I wanted to stay with Madr, that I was willing to give our mating a chance, and confessing I'd planned to flee from him the moment we reached the city.

All thoughts of what I should do fled when we

landed and the orcs melted from the woods around us, their weapons lifted.

Now I was scared.

An orc holding a lethal-appearing sword leaped toward us.

Madr jumped between us and lifted his staff, issuing his own challenge.

The male I assumed was from the Matis Clan tackled Madr, taking him to the ground. The two males rolled and came up to their feet, facing each other with their arms spread wide. The rest encircled us, trapping us.

An overwhelming urge to protect Madr surged inside me. Before I could rush toward them, intending to do something to help him, they tossed their weapons onto the ground and smacked their chests together, tusk-filled grins filling their faces.

"What are you doing here, Madr?" the other male asked while the rest crowded around them, smiling.

The two males embraced before parting.

I sagged against Brakkis. This was all . . . play?

"I came for the hunt," Madr said. He walked over to me and tugged me against his side, putting his arm around me. "This is my true mate, Lyneth. My pendant blazed for her."

"And it still blazes," the other male said with a low laugh, pointing to where it lit up his chest. "Why are you wasting time flying? You should be claiming your mate, making that pendant stop blinding the rest of us. No, you should be showing her the pleasure you can give her for the rest of her days."

I winced at how casually he spoke of intimacy. Thinking of all the wicked things I longed for Madr to do was much different than discussing them with a stranger.

"Lyneth, this is Dakur, caedos of the Matis Clan," Madr said. "We've been friends for a long time."

Dakur nodded, studying my face and frame, though not in a way that made me feel uncomfortable. Wearing only a leather loincloth, he was as handsome as Madr, strongly muscled and tall, though the hair swinging around his shoulders held hints of smoky lavender, unlike Madr's mossy green. He'd pulled it back, securing it at his neck.

"We saw Brakkis flying low and when you landed, we decided to say hello," Dakur said.

"My cousin stabbed Brakkis," Madr said. "We waited after the hunt for him to heal, which he thankfully has."

The males around us bristled, their grips tightening on their weapons.

"You killed Riank of course," Dakur said in a deadly voice.

"We initially fought after the hunt when he tried to claim my mate. I wounded him and believed that would be the end of it, but he injured my vox before he returned to the city. Believe me, I intend to seek vengeance."

I worried about him doing so. Would the other orcs allow him to attack Riank? I sensed there was something bigger going on here, though I had no idea what it might be.

Dakur snarled. "Riank assumed shaydes would kill you both, and he could then step into your place within the kingdom."

Madr scoffed, shooting a glance my way. "He has yet to win my father's approval. Eliminating me wouldn't bring that about any easier, especially if anyone suspected he was involved."

"You know the elders might insist he take your place if you're dead."

What place did Riank hope to claim? I looked between the two males, but nothing in their faces gave me a clue.

Madr shrugged. "There's plenty of time before we need to worry about that."

"From your mouth to the fates' ears." He peered past us to Brakkis. "He appeared to be flying well."

"His wing looks much better."

Dakur's gaze fell on me again, and I could read the puzzlement in his face.

"We only flew a short time," Madr said. "We'll let him rest and continue tonight when the shaydes hunt."

"Then you have time for a meal," Dakur said, his gaze taking in the sun still high in the sky. "I'd love to visit with you before you leave."

"Hunger gnaws on our bones." Madr dipped his head forward.

"Then we must feed your bellies to ensure your bones remain strong."

Was this a formal way of agreeing to dine with them?

Taking my hand, Madr squeezed it, and though a tic had appeared in his temple, indicting he could be tense, I didn't see any reason for me to be nervous. He'd said the Matis Clan was secretive. Were we about to learn a bit more about them?

"We'd be happy to join you," Madr added.

Dakur paused, looking at the males gathered around us, their hands on their weapons despite them being sheathed. They didn't watch us, however, but the woods around us.

Were we that unsafe even with so many together? I'd assumed we were secure sleeping with Brakkis nearby, but maybe Madr was the one who'd kept the shaydes away.

"We could prepare a meal here." Dakur gestured to the meadow around us. "Or you could join us in the trees. I'd be honored to share my fire with you."

CHAPTER 26

MADR

Few had met members of the Matis Clan, let alone joined any of them in their treetop homes.

"Will your vox be safe here?" Dakur asked. "I could leave some males with him. Two?" He lifted his pendant. "Allow me to call them."

I held up my hand. "No need. You know Brakkis. He could fight off a legion of shaydes. Now that he can fly, he won't need protection. If he leaves the meadow, he'll return at my call. But I thank you for your offer of protection."

"Very well." Dakur lifted his pendant again and blew across it, creating a low whistling sound. He was a master at this. I vaguely remembered he'd one time told me he wanted to be a wanderer, an orc who traveled to find new ways to use their pendants. "Then come with me, and my people will serve you a feast worthy of a prince."

A glance Lyneth's way showed she didn't seem to have noticed his mention of my former status in the kingdom. Or maybe she read his comment for how it was stated, not realizing he meant it literally.

I should've told her earlier. Why hadn't I? I would later.

Pivoting on his heel, Dakur strode toward the woods, pausing to speak with his males. They nodded and after studying me and my mate, half of them melted back into the woods, the rest staying with us.

Lyneth remained close beside me, almost clinging to my hand, shooting Dakur concerned looks. I wanted to reassure her, but Dakur would hear whatever I said. I trusted him, but this was his territory. We'd have to do what he asked if possible.

So all I could do was squeeze her hand and give her a tight smile.

Her tensioned loosened, and she sucked in a breath and released it.

"I've known Dakur for many years," I said as we entered the woods behind him. "We can trust him." More or less. This wasn't a hostage situation. He'd asked us to join him; he hadn't demanded it.

A few of his males strode ahead of us and one behind, while the rest entered the woods so silently, I could barely hear them. They disappeared, but that meant they'd be keeping us safe. Nothing would come near while the Matis clan protected us.

Dakur shot a glance over his shoulder, his appreciative gaze lingering on Lyneth. If we weren't good friends, I'd growl to warn him away.

"Madr and I played together when we were young," he said. "We battled first with wooden swords and then the real thing when we were ready. And we fought side by side when the dresalods attacked during one of my family's visits." He paused near an enormous tree, placing his feet on a section of the forest floor that appeared smoother than it should be.

He gestured for us to come close and stand with him, which we did.

With a hiss, the ground dropped away, sucking us down with it.

Lyneth gasped. I braced myself and lifted her into my arms, holding her tight. I'd suspected something like this, and the sparkle in Dakur's dark purple eyes told me he enjoyed being the one to deliver the surprise.

Before I had a chance to notice much more than a large room below the ground with tunnels leading in various directions, the circular area we stood on projected back up toward the forest surface at an incredible speed. It shot us up into the sky, and we soared between huge trees, into the canopy.

We landed lightly on wooden decking, and I placed Lyneth on her feet. She remained close beside me, shooting wide-eyed looks around us. We stood on a platform high in the trees with narrow bridges made up of vines and bobules around us.

Dakur shot me a grin. "Why aren't you gasping and clinging like your mate?"

I slapped his shoulder. "Because I know you, friend."

"You do." Dakur chuckled and teased his fingertip across Lyneth's chin. "Never fear, little one. You're completely safe with us and your mate." His attention returned to me. "However, because you have entered our territory, I won't be able to protect you completely."

For the first time, I frowned at him. Glared at him, actually, tightening my hand on my flail. I could pull it in a flash and use it, and he knew this. "What do you mean by that?"

"Your pendant still blazes."

"It won't for long."

"This means you haven't fully claimed her."

"I did so in the name of my clan the moment we met." Unease gouged through me.

"Others already know that she's still unmated. They saw this the moment you flew overhead."

Lyneth's gaze shot between us. As if she also sensed where this conversation was going, she pressed herself against my side, clinging to the tie of my loincloth.

"What are you saying, Dakur?" I growled.

His grim gaze met mine, and I read only sympathy there. "Others may challenge you for the chance to claim her."

"What does he mean by that?" I asked Madr, trying not to let panic come through in my voice. I got the impression I needed to project strength; not let on that I quivered inside.

"He means nothing by it," Madr snarled, his arm tightening around me. He lifted his staff, brandishing it. "We're leaving."

"I'd let you go if I could, but as I said, you landed in our territory, which means you were subject to our rules from that moment forward."

"You should've told me this back in the meadow. Then we would've left."

"Males surrounded you from the moment you landed. It wasn't until I was notified that I knew you were here. I'm sorry. I came as fast as I could. I hoped to avert what might happen." He shook his head, and I read the sympathy in his unusual lavender eyes. "I'll do all I can to intervene, and if we're fortunate, nothing will come of it."

"You're caedos," Madr said, and even I could hear death lurking in his words. "You have the final say."

"Only if someone doesn't—"

"I challenge you," someone said behind me and Madr.

We turned to find a male walking along two bands of vine stretched between the tree with our platform and another. His pendant, a five-star symbol with spikes on the tips flared, and his eyes remained on me.

"Finsteg," Dakur sighed. "Back away. Madr is our friend. He has claimed this female."

"Not fully." Finsteg's gaze never left me. "I have issued a challenge. Even as caedos, you have no say in this, not unless your pendant blazes as well."

Dakur growled, but I could tell he was as frustrated as Madr. "Very well. I hear and accept."

Finsteg stomped close to us and pressed his fist to his chest. "I, Finsteg, claim you, female, in the name of the Matis Clan."

"That's not possible," I hissed. They couldn't take me from Madr, could they?

Before Dakur or Madr could speak further, a second male leaped the distance between a tree to our left and this one, landing squarely on the flat wooden surface. He strode over to us, his gaze sliding down my frame. "She's small, but female. I'll make it work." His pendant also shone like a star that had shot down from above, though with lethal-appearing tips. "I, Pulost, claim you in the name of the Matis Clan."

Dakur held up his hand and lifted his voice. "No more. So I say, so it shall be. Enough challenges have been issued."

"What are you doing?" Madr barked at Dakur.

Bracing Madr's shoulders, Dakur sighed. "I'm sorry, friend. When I realized you hadn't fully claimed her, and my males knew this, I brought you here hoping to present you as a guest. I hoped that would prevent challenges."

"What's going on?" I cried, more in anger than dismay. I didn't like how the two other males looked at me as if I was a prize to be won with the sleight of their hand.

Or a declaration.

"Madr has not yet fully claimed you," Dakur told me. "For many generations, in my clan, males fought for the right to claim mates."

"You said your pendant chose me," I told Madr.

"It did," he bit out.

Dakur looked between us. "When a female states her intention to mate, it's common among my clan for the clan fates to choose more than one male. They fight to decide who is the worthiest." Sorrow came through in his voice, and I read the dismay in his eyes when he looked my way. "I apologize to both of you, but there isn't much even I, as caedos, am allowed to do. All I can do was limit the challengers." He grunted to the males.

"We will deal with this in two hours. Go, prepare yourselves."

The two males nodded, their attention remaining on me for a moment before they swung to Madr. They *assessed* him.

They sharply pivoted and sprang away, one swinging on a vine to another tree, the second dropping all the way to the ground. When he landed, he raced into the underbrush.

"I'm sorry," Dakur said softly. "I did all I could."

Madr growled. "I'm not subject to your rules."

"In your prior role? No. But you relinquished it. When you revoked your position in the kingdom, you changed the path you walk on." His attention swung to me. "Does she know of your past?"

"No," Madr sighed.

"Why not?"

"It isn't important any longer."

"I'd say it is." Dakur's lips thinned. "Now you're a regular citizen of the orc kingdom. As such, you're subject to the rules of wherever you plant your feet. In this case, you landed your vox in my clan's territory. My clan's fates were able to intervene from that very moment."

Madr shook his head. "Two have challenged me."

"You're saying you have to battle them to claim me?" I asked, seeing where this was going.

"He does," Dakur said. "By not solidifying his claim

with you, he has opened himself up to new challenges. Now he must fight to solidify his claim."

"He has to do this because we haven't had sex?" I barked. "That shouldn't matter. He claimed me in the name of his clan, and I'm claiming him. I, Lyneth, claim you, Madr, as mine, in the name of the ... Willar clan. My family name." Did he know Rhoslyn's last name? He didn't flinch or give any indication the name meant anything to him, so she may not have mentioned it. "You're mine, and I'm yours."

His arm tightened around me. Turning me in his embrace, he cupped my face gently with his big hands, his gaze meeting mine. I read so much sorrow there; it gutted me.

I whimpered, and he stroked my cheeks with his thumbs.

"I have to do this," he said softly. "I have no choice."

"There's always a choice. Tell them no. We can run. Grab me and jump to the ground. We'll run to Brakkis and take flight, leaving this nightmare behind."

"We cannot."

"Why?"

"He would dishonor his name and clan," Dakur said softly. "No orc would ever do such a thing."

"But you could be killed," I cried out. "I can't bear to lose you, Madr."

"Mate." He leaned forward and kissed me, and I read so much longing there. It made my pulse sing and my heart split in two. "Trust me in this?"

I nodded. "I do. Always, Madr."

He flashed me a tusk-filled grin, though it held a hint of sadness. "You claimed me, mate, and that means everything." He pressed his fist against his chest. "Know in my heart that I'm yours forever."

Dakur released a high-pitched cry, and it was answered from all directions, as if the tops of the trees had come alive with orcs.

"Come, Lyneth," he said. "You'll remain with me while they complete the challenges." He nodded to Madr. "I'll protect her with everything I have. You've been a brother to me all my life. She's now the sister I never had."

"I'll be with you soon, my sweet." Madr kissed me again quickly.

Spinning, he leaped off the platform, landing squarely on the ground. His staff in hand, he ran into the woods without looking back.

CHAPTER 28

MADR

L yneth had claimed me, and under normal circumstances, I wouldn't be happier. My precious mate. I couldn't wait to tell her I loved her. But first, I'd have to defend my right to claim her one final time.

I'd barely reached the woods when a male stepped onto the path ahead of me.

"I'm Zickar," he said, studying my frame.

"Madr."

He tilted his head to his left. "Come with me. I'll help you prepare."

He pivoted and jogged down the trail with me right behind. I'd only vaguely heard about Matis Clan challenges. It wasn't anything done by my clan or those in the vicinity of the orc city. Another mystery about the Matis Clan, one I'd no doubt be asked to swear never to discuss. Lyneth, too.

I wasn't too worried about losing any challenge they could give me. First, I trusted the fates. They'd made my pendant blaze for Lyneth first. I loved her, and she'd just claimed me. They wouldn't tear us apart.

Second, I could thank my father for insisting I train from the time I could pick up a sword. He'd hired the best to teach me, and now I'd put those skills to the ultimate test. Still, it never paid to underestimate an enemy. For now, that was who they were, males who'd take my mate from me if they could.

Zickar stopped at a smooth circle on the forest floor and gestured for me to join him. Would this one project us upward or would we sink down and remain there?

The moment I'd stepped onto the surface beside him, we dropped quickly and were engulfed by the earth. The platform didn't bottom out until it had sunk at least four or five levels beneath the surface. It came to a smooth halt, and Zickar stepped off, striding down a long hallway channeled through the dirt. I followed; my footsteps were nearly silent on the smooth flat stones embedded in the soil beneath me.

At the end of the corridor, we reached a four-way intersection, and he turned right. Reaching a wooden door, he opened it and gestured for me to enter ahead of him.

I stepped into a dark chamber where the roar of water echoed around me.

Following me inside, Zickar grunted.

Despite my excellent night vision, I could barely see

him standing beside me. He lifted his pendant to his lips and blow across it, creating a low humming sound.

Lights bloomed around us, and I gaped at the enormous chamber made up of smooth stone walls and spears of rock plunging down from the ceiling at least three stories above. A broad pool took up most of the cavern, gleaming pale lavender in the light of the whisps coating the ceiling and stone spears high above.

"We blow on our whisps themselves to make them ignite," I said, taking in the narrow falls plunging down a series of slopes on the opposite side of the cave. Water frothed and foamed when it hit the pool, and a lavender mist floated across the surface.

"We've taught them to respond to our pendants," Zickar said.

"My pendant doesn't do that." I lifted it and blew but didn't make a sound.

Zickar chuckled.

"How did you create a sound with yours?"

His grin widened, his tusks gleaming white in the light. "It's a clan secret I won't share."

"Fair enough."

"You must remove your clothing. You need to purify yourself before you'll be allowed to answer the challenges."

I stripped quickly. "I'll bathe?"

"You must swim all the way across the pool and stand beneath the falls." He turned and headed toward the door. "When you've finished, there will be a drying cloth and a fresh garment waiting for you back here." He opened the door but paused in the entrance. "Ignore them. They won't cause you harm."

He left before I could question him further.

I looked up at the whisps. In the city, our whisps would generate light for at least an hour from one puff of air. How long would a sound made across a clan pendant keep them glowing?

Hopefully long enough to reach the falls and return.

Striding to the edge of the pool, I peered down through the crystal-clear water, taking in boulders far below, plus wavering dark purple grasses.

Something large shifted down there, but I couldn't quite make it out.

A dresalod? No, they lived in the salty sea, and . . . Stooping down, I cupped some water and tasted it. No salt.

With a sharp nod, I dove into the water.

I swam briskly across the pool, not slowing until I reached the falls. After climbing boulders near the base of the falls, I stood atop the highest and let the water pummel me. It felt good, like I'd talked someone into giving me a massage, something my father commonly did. Not me. I'd never felt comfortable closing my eyes and letting someone run their hands across my body.

Lyneth was welcome to do so if she wished.

If I hadn't dealt with attempts on my life pretty much all my life, I might feel differently about what I faced.

At least I'd grow up with Jaus nearby. We'd watched

each other's backs in addition to training together. My father had only reluctantly allowed him inside the palace training rooms; I suspected Jaus's mother insisted. But my father forbade Jaus from entering the classrooms, and he certainly hadn't invited my brother to dine at our table or sit with us in areas reserved for family.

Because I loved my brother, I felt bad about what I was given, and he was denied. And I blamed our father.

Spying a cloth and bar of soap on a rock nearby, I used them to bathe, savoring how good it felt to be clean once more. Battle would bring out my sweat, and if the Matis warriors fought as well as the palace guards—and I was confident they did—I'd soon be covered in grime.

Zickar returned with a garment in his hand and waved, indicating it was time for me to return to the other side of the pool.

After rinsing off the soap, I dove into the water once more, swimming quickly across the open expanse.

I'd nearly reached the opposite side when something latched onto my ankle and dragged me below the surface.

CHAPTER 29

LYNETH

Dakur led me to a span of vines stretching from this tree to another and started across, placing his feet on the two that shifted and stretched while holding onto the others at waist-level. Thinner vines connected the two he stepped on, but there was nothing to stop me from slipping off one and plunging past them to the ground.

He paused when I didn't follow. "Would you like me to carry you?"

The thought of dangling over his shoulder while he made his way across frightened me more than the thought of losing my balance.

If I wasn't so frightened about what might happen to Madr, my shrill laugh would ring out.

"I'm fine." I waved for him to continue and with a deep breath, I stepped out onto the vine on the right. It held my weight, as did the one on the left. Clinging to the "railing" vines, I moved slowly behind him. "Fun."

He chuckled. "You're doing well for your first time."

"My life has been a series of firsts lately."

"All good, I hope."

I grinned and loosened my fingers on the vines I clung to. "Very good."

"Madr is a good mate for you. He's a wonderful person, but even more, he makes you happy." He didn't make that a question, but I nodded as if he had.

"I'm falling in love with him." I surprised myself by stating this. Another first for me.

"As you should."

I huffed. "As I *wish*. There's no should in this."

"When a clan pendant picks, which Madr's has, you're destined to love each other forever." His voice came out wistful.

"Has your pendant picked someone for you?"

"Sadly, no. And I haven't had time to go to the hunt for a few years. My father was murdered, leaving me to assume rule of the clan, and there hasn't been time for a mate yet. I hope to attend the hunt soon, however." He lifted his gaze to the canopy above. "The fates have waited, but I sense they grow impatient."

"Only two women are sent from the village each year."

He shot me a grin. "And when I attend next, one of them will be mine."

He was conceited, but that appeared to be a common

orc trait. "Maybe you'll need to go many years before one causes your pendant to light up."

"Maybe." He shrugged. "That's for another time. Next year or the one after that. She'll wait for me."

"Perhaps your pendant will ignite for a male."

"I welcome whoever the fates send me, male or female."

"This makes me wonder why it's always women who must be sent to the hunt. Why not males?"

"We didn't specify in our treaty."

I gasped, and he spun, his hand snapping out to grab my arm, but I wasn't freezing or falling, and nothing was attacking me. I'd forgotten all about how high off the ground I was and how feeble the vines felt beneath my shoes. His words had stolen my breath.

"You. Didn't. Specify?" I bit out.

"I assume from your reaction that they told you only women must be sent each year."

"Damn men." I stomped my foot, anger making my body burn.

"I agree." His low chuckle rang out. "Damn men. You must tell them this."

"I doubt I'll return." They didn't want me.

Madr did.

"I'll find a way to send a message." Would they believe me? Probably not. My growl ripped out. "Fuck them," I shouted.

"Yes, fuck them." His unusual purple eyes sparkled.

"As for who my pendant will pick, I'm confident it will find a way."

He seemed sweet. Stoic and bound by duty, yet fair to those he encountered.

I joined him on yet another platform, this one peppered with small buildings.

"Sometimes we sleep here," he said, opening the door to the first.

"Sometimes?" I was so angry with my village, but I had to put it aside. I'd find a way to deal with it later.

"Yes, that's it. And sometimes, we sleep elsewhere."

"You're a mysterious clan."

He grinned. "That's correct."

We stepped inside a single wooden-walled room holding a bed and a tub in the corner. Lavendar steam drifted off the water, telling me it was hot.

I bit back my groan of anticipation.

"I sent word ahead for someone to prepare this room for you." Dakur waved to the gown lying on the bed. "Feel welcome to wash and change your clothing. Eat from the tray of food I also arranged to have sent for you."

It sat on a low table near the bed.

"We won't dine again until after the challenge has finished," he added. "Then, we'll celebrate your mating with the winner."

I lifted my chin and met his gaze with ire churning through me. "You can't force me to be with someone just because they win the challenge. That's what the village did to me, and damn, but I'm not letting anyone decide my future for me but myself."

"I don't blame you for feeling angry. But what about Madr?"

"In my heart, he's already my mate."

"I'm sure the clan fates know this. Pray they guide his success in the challenge."

And if he didn't win? I wasn't going to think about that unless I had to, but I wouldn't lie with a random orc no matter what the fates decided.

"I can send a female to help you undress if you have need," Dakur said.

The time I needed help undressing was the time I laid down and let the fates claim me. "I can do it alone."

"As you wish. Leave your soiled clothing on the bed. They'll be cleaned and returned to you before you depart in the morning."

"You're confident Madr will win the challenges, or you wouldn't have mentioned me leaving." Despite my irritation with the village elders, I could barely stop thinking about Madr—worrying about him.

"I trust the judgement of the fates," was all he said as he backed from the room and shut the door.

I rushed over to it and swung it open, grateful to find it wasn't locked, though I wasn't sure why he'd need to pen me inside.

Dakur was gone, of course, though who knew where. Leaves rustled around me, but that could be from the wind.

I didn't dare venture across a bridge alone and the ground was too far down to jump. The thought of climbing down made my legs shake. Even if I reached the surface, I didn't know where I could run to other than to Brakkis, but in what direction?

Shaydes would hunt me like they had my parents.

Besides, I'd never leave Madr.

Backing into the room, I shut the door and stripped quickly. After placing the tray of food near the tub, I sunk down into the water with a heady sigh. Amazing. Back in the village, a poor person's options for bathing included the river or a small basin in our room. Breaking the ice on the river in the winter didn't improve the temperature. I'd only felt truly clean when washing there, and it had to be done quickly in case spying eyes peered from the woods.

I nibbled on bread, meat, and cheese, washing it down with a lightly floral ale that soon made my head spin.

Remembering what Dakur told me about the treaty, I growled.

"Damn men," I said to the room in general. "How could they do this to us?"

Using a cloth left on a low table beside the tub, plus the bar of sweetly scented soap, I first washed my hair, then my body, groaning at how wonderfully luxurious this felt.

Sometime later, the tray was empty, and the water had started to cool. I'd also set aside my anger, though I still planned to do something about this. I just have to figure out what.

I stepped out of the water, dried, and dressed in the gown that fit fairly well. Someone was good at judging sizes. Surely it couldn't be Dakur, though I'd seen no other orcs other than the two males who appeared to think they stood a chance of claiming me.

I combed my hair and pulled it back, not wanting to deal with it right now.

When I stepped outside, a female orc was waiting.

She gave me a shy smile. "I'm Sessavia. Our caedos asked me to wait here for you and bring you to the central meeting place once you'd finished."

I nodded, smiling too. "I'm Lyneth."

"Welcome to the Matis Clan."

"Thank you. You've all been gracious." Well, other than the males who wished to claim me.

"We don't see visitors often." She waved for me to follow her past the other small buildings to the far side, where another vine bridge stretched farther than I could see. "Did you have enough to eat?"

"Yes, thank you."

"That's good, then. Come. I'll take you to our caedos." She stepped easily out onto the bridge like she was walking on a leaf-strewn ground, glancing back with merriment in her eyes. "You must be excited about the upcoming challenges. Imagine. Three! So many choices. Soon, your new mate will claim you. We've prepared a special place for the occasion."

"Excuse me?"

Pausing, she turned and leaned back against one of the waist-high vines. It bowed from her movement, and it was all I could do not to grab her arm and haul her upright once more. Surely, it wouldn't break. Surely, she wouldn't fall.

"I speak of the mating rush that occurs when one of them wins the challenge and claims you fully, solidifying your mating."

"Tonight?"

Her smile widened. "Yes, tonight."

I wasn't going to think about being with anyone but Madr. "I have a mate already. Madr."

She shrugged; her expression solemn but resigned. "He should've claimed you fully the moment you met."

I was anything but resigned. "Don't you want to get to know the person before you do . . . that?"

With a soft laugh, she continued across the great expanse, confidently placing her feet on the vines. "If our clan chooses him for me, then yes. I'd welcome his embrace. I know I'll soon love him."

I sighed and followed. "I was married once. Mated, that is."

"Then you know the joy that can be found with a mate."

"He wasn't chosen for me by my pendant or anything like that."

"I've heard humans do the choosing—or a person's parents." She sent me a pursed-lipped look. "Imagine such horror. How would they know who you're most compatible with?"

"Perhaps it's the same thing as a pendant choosing?"

"Never," she vowed. "I cannot imagine my family randomly selecting a mate for me. How would they know any better than me who will best fit?"

"Yet you trust your pendants."

"The fates guide them," she said smugly. "Unlike a parent who might be guided by greed or the wish to cater to a certain family."

She was wise.

Finally, we reached the end of the long bridge, and while my legs shook from adrenaline and struggling to maintain my footing with the sway of the vines, I felt proud of my ability to do this. Like with Madr's vox, I was taking on new challenges and coming up the victor.

Perhaps it was time for me to spread my wings further.

After crossing three long bridges, we arrived at a big open platform. Dakur sat in a large, intricately scrolled wooden chair, speaking with a few other males. A smaller chair had been placed beside his and the only other female in sight, an elderly orc, perched on the edge.

Her milky gaze turned my way when I stepped off the bridge. Was she blind?

She held out her hand and one of the males took it, helping her out of the chair and leading her carefully over to me. She walked slowly and with a hunched, twisted spine, plus a pronounced limp.

"Tenkaril would like to touch your face if you will allow this," Sessavia said from beside me. "She's our wisest elder, and she sees all."

Maybe she wasn't blind, then?

"Wise I may or may not be, but Sessavia is correct," Tenkaril said in a creaky voice. A tusky smile flashed across her face. "I sometimes see what others do not and they have turned this into a legend when they shouldn't have."

I was more confused now than I'd been before her introduction.

"Please feel welcome to touch my face," I said, my body stiffening. In the village, older people were revered and cherished. It appeared Matis Clan orcs treated this elder the same.

But that didn't mean I was comfortable with strangers touching me.

"What is seen cannot be unseen," Tenkaril said, her brow tightening.

"You foretell the future?" I asked, taking a step backward, bumping into Sessavia.

"That's not correct." Tenkaril shook her head. Her bunched up grayed hair still streaked with lavender shifted on the back of her skull. "I *see*."

Chills shot through me, but this was harmless, right? She was a wise elder and obviously well respected in the clan. She'd touch me, sputter a few sentences that could be interpreted in many ways, then return to her chair beside Dakur.

I swallowed and decided to hold still for as long as this took. "Please, feel welcome," I said again, my voice the croaky one now.

Sessavia's hand landed on my lower back, nudging me forward.

Tenkaril lifted her wrinkled hands and carefully placed them on my cheeks with the thumbs poised above my eyes. "Closed," she snapped.

I lowered my eyelids, shutting out the world around us, leaving me sightless—like Tenkaril.

The scent of damp earth swirled in my sinuses, as well as a light floral perfume that could come from blossoms nearby or Tenkaril herself. Birds cheeped in the canopy above, their wings fluttering. Someone on the platform shuffled his feet and coughed, and someone else released gas.

I hoped I didn't get to smell that too.

She stroked her thumbs across my eyelids, muttering something in a language I hadn't heard before. Ancient orc?

"Ah, yes. I see," she mumbled. "Very interesting." She released my face and stepped back.

I cautiously opened my eyes, and they met hers.

"He watches," she said. "Not here. He wouldn't dare. But elsewhere. Take care, or you could lose what is most precious."

"What does that mean?" I asked.

Tenkaril held her hand out to her left and the male

who'd assisted her before guided her back to the chair, where she sat.

Sessavia leaned close behind me, whispering by my ear. "You're so fortunate. She sees for so few nowadays."

"I'm honored," I said just as softly. "Truly. But what she said doesn't make much sense."

"It will. In time, it will."

CHAPTER 30

MADR

Choking, I floundered while whatever had latched onto me sucked me down, down, down until my feet hit the bottom of the pool.

My eyes open, I glared at the long, scaled creature that had grabbed me.

So much for nothing paying me any attention.

The beast dragged me across the bottom of the pool, and I reached for a rock, lifting it and bringing it down as hard as I could on the limb wrapped around my ankle.

With a muffled groan, the creature spun its upper body around. Its mouth opened, revealing teeth as long as my fingers and a gaping maw big enough to swallow me whole.

I bashed the rock against the side of its head, and it reared back. It released my leg with a snap and floundered across the bottom of the pool, sliding into an opening along the side.

Before another could take up where this one left off, I swam to the surface, and clutching the rock, made my way out of the pool.

Zickar grunted. "Never seen one of them do that before."

"I must've looked tasty."

He snorted. "Or an easy mark."

I lifted one brow. "I'm never easy."

He slapped my shoulder. "We'll see how you feel come morning."

"What do you mean by that?" Grabbing the cloth, I dried myself, then dressed in the clean loincloth, securing the tie at the side of my waist. I strapped the sheath with my flail onto my back.

"Winning versus losing." He turned to the door. "You never know how it'll come out, but if you're the winner, I imagine you'll feel great in the morning."

"I haven't lost a match since I was ten outside of a few to my older brother, and he had to fight hard to best me."

"You've fought a Matis?" he asked as we left the cavern and traveled back to the transport device that projected us back up to the surface.

"Your caedos and I have sparred in the past."

"I imagine he was soft with you. He wouldn't wish to injure a prince."

So Dakur had shared my true identity, at least with Zickar.

"I'm no longer a prince. I'm plain old Madr now."

Zickar grunted as he strode in the opposite direction of where I'd left Lyneth, taking a trail through the woods. "I doubt there's anything plain about you. And while you may have rejected your role in your clan, that doesn't mean you no longer wear the cloak."

"I shed it," I stated. "Dropped it onto the ground with no intention of donning it again."

"You'll let your cousin pick it up and wear it instead?"

"Dakur shared more than he should."

"Don't we all." He started across a bridge, and I followed. "I'll give you one hint about the challenge."

"I appreciate that."

He glanced over his shoulder but kept striding forward. "It won't involve battle."

"I don't need to fight them to the death? That's how it would go in my clan."

"Each clan member is precious. Few are scorned or sent away. Expressing a wish to claim a mate when your pendant has flared is not something that should result in banishment or death."

"Wise."

"Here in the forest, there are enough things trying to kill us. We don't need to do so ourselves."

"What kind of challenge will I face, then?"

"That, I cannot tell you."

"Another clan secret?"

"No one is allowed to know prior to the match. You'll face it along with them."

We left the trail, emerging out into a meadow ringed by trees. Zickar directed me to the center, where the other two males waited.

The sound of voices drew my eye to a platform built into the side of one of the tallest trees.

Lyneth stood there with Dakur, looking down.

When our gazes met, my heart tightened. She was dressed in a new gown, and she appeared well.

I trusted Dakur to keep her safe, but who would protect her if I lost the upcoming challenge?

CHAPTER 31

MADR

Dakur blew across his pendant, creating a low hum that resonated in my bones. The sound faded, and Zickar nodded.

"The first to complete his course will be declared the victor," he told me softly. "There are no rules other than you are not allowed to attack one of the others. If you win, and I have faith in your skills, Madr, you will do so because you are more agile and quicker than the others."

Their pendants blazed, as did mine, and I looked up, my gaze meeting Lyneth's again.

I couldn't stand the thought of never seeing her—touching her—again. While banishment was not common in the Matis Clan, I was not Matis. I'd be sent from here the moment I lost, and she'd remain behind. I could gnash my tusks and snarl, and even try to sneak back into this clan's territory to rescue her, but it would serve no purpose. This was a Matis challenge, and I, a

Lumen warrior, must answer with the best of my ability.

I must also agree to abide by the result. There could be no outcome but my win.

I nodded Zickar's way. "Thank you."

He braced my shoulders and grinned. "The fates will supposedly choose, but I suspect they already have."

My grunt rang out. I'd trust my clan's fates. They'd never take me in the wrong direction. Lyneth was mine, and I'd prove it to them all.

Zickar stepped away and strode over to stand in front of the three of us. The other two looked me over, and one sneered, though he said nothing. They'd been raised here; they knew the forest much better than me.

But I loved Lyneth. That would drive me to win. It would surpass their abilities.

"Challenges have been issued," Zickar said loudly, and a murmur echoed from those watching in the canopy around us. I sensed many, though most were hidden among the leaves.

I glanced up once more, memorizing Lyneth's face in case this was the last time I saw it.

"Whoever finishes the course first will claim the mate chosen by his pendant," Zickar said. "Each course is identical and runs parallel to the others. The first section is made up of shifting platforms." His attention slid to me but only for a moment.

I was grateful he was sharing what he could.

"In the second, you must pass through an avestilar

village," he said. "Remember, the enormous creatures do not enjoy being disturbed, and they will attack."

What was an avestilar?

As if one heard my thought, a shrill caw rang out above and some distance ahead. The canopy actually *swayed* as something moved through it. A large bird, then? I'd soon find out.

"The third part of the challenge involves solitary vine bridges."

Finsteg grunted, and his gaze met Pulost's. They wouldn't work together, naturally. They couldn't if we each had our own course to follow. And they'd both be eager to win. While I'd heard there were females here, I suspected there weren't as many as males. Had the shaydes killed here as well?

The chance to mate with a clan-chosen female rarely came more than once in a person's lifetime. Why had the fates given them the chance to claim Lyneth?

These two had lived in the treetops their entire lives. They probably saw the other male as their sole competition and me someone to scorn.

I'd prove them wrong.

"Can you tell me more about the solitary vine bridges?" I asked.

Finsteg grinned, as did Pulost.

"Cross them fast," Finsteg said.

Pulost released a mocking chuckle. "Very fast."

"Too fast, and you will fall, and you could be injured," Zickar said. "That part of the challenge also involves agility and skill. As for the fourth, your task is to find a way across the open chasm between one tree and the last."

What did that mean? I suspected from Finsteg and Pulost's stunned looks, this section might prove to be the hardest section.

"No weapons will be needed here," Zickar said. The three of us tossed them on the ground. "They'll wait for you at the end of the course." His gaze scanned the three of us. "Ready?" At our nods, he waved to nearby trees marked with bright red ribbons. "Choose a course."

We each strode over to a tree. I looked up, studying the branches of the one I'd selected, plus the platforms far above the ground. The platforms extended beyond the tree but shifted and twisted, tipping and gliding in all directions. They resembled the surfaces the Matis Clan used to travel deep below the ground and up into the canopy, though I didn't see one close that I could use to ascend.

I'd climb, then.

I nodded to Zickar, as did the other two.

He lifted his pendant and after sucking in a deep breath, he blew across it, generating a high-pitched squeal.

CHAPTER 32

MADR

As I stood beneath the tree, the forest echoed with the cries of birds and the low hum of insects.

My heart thrummed with determination. I had to win; I wouldn't finish this without claiming my mate. A glance at Finsteg and Pulost told me the same fire gleamed in their eyes.

My gaze lifted to the series of floating platforms I must first overcome, hovering high above like precarious stepping stones leading toward victory. The wind whispered through the leaves as Dakur blew across his pendant, creating a low hum.

Begin.

Adrenaline surged through me as I leaped up, grasping a low branch on my designated tree. Muscles straining against gravity's pull, I continued climbing while keeping an eye on the wobbling platforms. As they swayed and shifted, they'd test my agility. A fall might not kill me, but I'd not only lose my momentum, but I could also be injured badly enough that I couldn't continue the course.

I reached the highest branch possible and studied the first platform as it glided in my direction. Flat and smooth, it appeared to have been constructed of metal, though I couldn't imagine where the Matis Clan could find such a thing. They appeared to live simply; their homes crafted from materials grown in the world around them.

When the platform started gliding away from the tree I stood on, I jumped. My foot landed true on the surface even as it dipped precariously downward. A hop launched me onto the next island suspended in mid-air.

Each jump required focus—my instinctive balance honed by years spent training with the best the orc kingdom had to offer.

I hadn't been raised among ancient trees whispering secrets from long ago, but I'd been educated further than many. Playing with my brother and other orclings in the city streets had turned me into a worthy opponent.

Strong gusts of wind raced between branches overhead as I leaped and flung myself from one platform to another, my gaze periodically caught by the brilliant purple foliage below.

Finally, I reached the end of the course, jumping

what felt like the length of a tree to make it, landing hard on my abdomen on a wooden platform where a member of the Matis Clan waited, watching me stoically.

I grinned as I jumped to my feet, but my excitement dropped quickly when I saw Finsteg and Pulost already partway through the next part of the challenge.

Determined to catch up and pass them, I charged across the wooden platform and into the next phase—a series of enormous trees with clay and stick birdhouses strewn among the thick upper branches.

I flung myself upward, grabbing onto a branch and pulling myself up to stand on the bark's surface. A bird-house perched on a limb on the opposite side of the tree, and it appeared the only way I could progress through the course would be to climb over the mud and stick structure.

I couldn't see anything inside the nest through the hole in the side. Did a female sit on eggs in the darkness or were the parents hunting for their avestilar young?

Balancing on treacherous limbs just wide enough for my bare feet, I navigated the tangled maze of sticks and leaves, working my way along the branch, around the trunk, and up onto the nest taller and broader than me.

A cry high above made my pulse roar, and the swoop of wings grew louder. A bird dove through the canopy, a mass of purple feathers streaked with gold. Its equally golden beak opened as it approached with claws extended.

Damn, it had teeth.

I flung myself forward and landed hard on the top of the nest. Not pausing, I scrambled to my feet and leaped from the top of this nest, across the small expanse between this tree and the next, and landed feet first on top of another nest, the faint scent of resin mingling with the earthly musk of rotting leaves far below.

My pulse raced as wings flapped louder. A glance behind showed three of the birds heading my way. Their shrill squawks sent chills across my bones.

The bird in the lead lunged toward me, gnashing its teeth. Its claws raked across my shoulder, and I bit back a cry.

I flung myself onto a branch below and raced to the end, jumping to the next tree with an even larger flock not far behind me. Determination etched itself into my very being. I would finish this course, and I'd do so in the lead.

Branches shook beneath me when I landed on them, but I refused to slow my pace or pause to battle the birds. I picked where I placed my feet quickly, and kept going, climbing over one nest after another.

I was rewarded when I landed squarely on another wooden platform, finding the same Matis clansmale waiting. He nodded and gave me a quick grin, gesturing to my opponents who were still making their way across their courses.

Halfway, and I was finally ahead.

I scanned the next section I had to complete as quickly as I could. I had momentum, and I couldn't risk losing it. A series of solitary bands of vines stretched from one tree to another. I'd have to cross them all.

Without pausing any longer, I dashed forward, leaping and landing squarely on the first strand of vine connecting this tree to the next.

The bridge swayed beneath my weight, and without a vine railing to grab onto, I flung my arms out to maintain my balance. At least the vines didn't shift and twist —so far.

My heart pounded against my ribs as I focused on maintaining control, making my way along the taut vine that sloped up toward the next tree, then the vine after that.

In no time, I'd crossed five vines and reached a tiny platform, where I paused long enough to study the next vine I had to cross. Then the one after that. From here, it appeared I still had three to traverse before I reached the final platform where the same clansmale now waited. How had he crossed the span so fast? Vines dangling higher above told me he might've swung.

My two competitors weren't far behind me. A glance to my right showed them one and two vines back.

Sweat trickled down my forehead and the weight of countless eyes watched me from platforms mounted along the sides of the course. Only a low murmur of voices reached me; most remained silent. How many lived in the Matis Clan? I'd never asked Dakur, but now, I wanted to know.

I carefully balanced my weight as I stepped onto a vine bridge, its slimy surface shifting beneath my feet. The forest canopy stretched out below me, a mesmerizing sea of varying shades of purple. The bridge sloped up and down between the trees, which would make it difficult to maintain stability. I focused on each step, taking care not to lose my footing.

Approaching the end of this vine, I growled when I saw that a section was nearly missing. Only a thread too unstable to stand on stretched between the fragments. How did the vine remain in place with this break? I wasn't sure, but when I placed my foot on the thin section, it bowed downward. I'd be a fool to trust it.

Without hesitation, I took a deep breath and leaped forward. The better section of vine swayed beneath my weight, and I worried the entire thing would snap, but I kept going until I reached the tree. Perched on a branch, I studied the next vine before stepping out onto it.

A gust of wind whipped through the treetops, threatening to send me flying. My heart thumped like thunder as I balanced on the vine, bending low against its forceful push.

The next challenge was squeezing through narrow gaps between trees without getting entangled in thick branches and thorn patches. The air grew thicker here with an earthy scent mixed with damp moss and decaying leaves. Balancing myself precariously on the vine near a gap only wide enough for my body's width ahead, I slowly worked myself forward while avoiding sharp thorns. A squitt squawked nearby, and I froze, but the tiny creature wasn't a threat. It threw a nut my way, but it bounced off my chest. When I released a low snarl, it took off, leaving only swaying leaves behind.

If it had been a shayde, I'd pay more attention.

Next came a steep decline—a rush of adrenaline surged through me as I half-slid down the incline. At the base, still well above the ground, the vine connected with a metal ring the size of my fist. A new vine stretched sharply up away from the ring, toward another tree. My leg muscles twitched with exhaustion, pushed beyond their limits.

Late day sunlight sliced through dense foliage above, casting shifting patterns along the vine and the area around me, playing tricks with my mind.

I moved past the ring and upward, finally reaching the top of the vine, where I clung to the trunk and gave my body a short break. My shoulders burned and my breath came in ragged gasps, but a sense of accomplishment surged through me as I raced across the final—and straight—vine, landing solidly on the wooden platform beside the same Matis clansmale.

"One challenge left," he said, dipping his head forward in a bow. His gaze shot past me, and a glance toward Finsteg and Pulost showed both making their way up the final incline.

I wiped sweat from my brow with the back of my

hand and intently studied the last part of the trial, seeing no vine to cross, no rope or projectile platform. The expanse between here and the tree where a group of orcs —and Lyneth—waited was much too far to jump. A glance overhead showed the trees didn't connect, so I couldn't climb higher to find a shorter distance.

An enormous hilardep had built a nest high above in this tree. The female spider the size of an orc wasn't in view, but I was confident the venomous creature waited somewhere nearby, hidden in the canopy. Local squitts should be wary since they were her easiest prey, though she wouldn't be opposed to biting and entrapping a small orc if they got stuck in the rope-strong webbing.

An inky pool stretched across the entire open ground far below, and while a person might be able to swim across it, more often than not, creatures lurked beneath the surface of such pools, waiting. I wasn't keen on being dragged down into the black mud.

The clansmale watched me, but I was sure he wouldn't be allowed to give me hints for completing the final part of the course.

As Finsteg landed on decking nearby, finishing the vine challenge, I peered around frantically, looking for a way across but seeing nothing.

Wait.

I peered up at the hilardep nest, studying the webbing. I'd heard it was strong enough to hold a struggling orc.

Pulost landed on a nearby platform and sent us snarls.

I had to do something. Now.

Grabbing onto the branch above me, I pulled myself up. I continued climbing, keeping a wary eye on the web cluster. The spider wouldn't hesitate to attack if she thought she could grab me, stun me, and quickly wrap me in her web.

I slowed my pace as I approached the broad web taking up a big section of the canopy, squinting through the muted sunlight but still not seeing the spider.

Moving slowly and carefully, I reached up, my fingers brushing against the outer edge of the hilardep web. I held my breath and tore it away from its perch, coiling it around my hand. The silk felt rough against my calloused palms, and I hoped it would be strong enough for my plan. I couldn't think of any other way to finish the course.

Slowly, I tugged more of it away from the main web, avoiding the strands that gleamed with a sticky coating. In a few places, I had to break the web and knot my strand to one without the gleaming substance she'd use to trap her prey.

A shadow slunk across the canopy above. She'd felt the pull and was coming to investigate.

I held my breath as I gathered more web, dragging it in faster now that I was close to being discovered.

"Are you a fool?" Finsteg hissed from nearby. "She'll eat you."

Pulost snorted. "Leave him to be caught. Her bite will make sure we have less competition." He peered around, seeking a way across the broad expanse. "I'm going down." A leap, and he landed squarely on the ground. He approached the inky pool cautiously and looked on either side, seeking a way around it, but I'd already noted the swampy area stretched for many cliks in either direction. Even at a dead run, it would take too long to work my way around the swamp.

Finsteg huffed and began climbing his tree, working his way to the higher branches where he'd be closer to our destination. The web stretching from my tree across the tops of theirs shook, and the shadowy spider hissed.

Fuck.

I pulled faster, gathering more web.

She leaped, landing on a branch above Finsteg, and he froze, peering up at her. Now that he was no longer moving, her four-eyed gaze swept past him and landed hard on me. Her pale lavender fur bristled, and she tightened her six claws on the branch beneath her. She tipped her head back and shot webbing up. It hit another branch extending between that tree and mine and flipped around it, securing it in place.

She was going to use it to reach me.

With my heart pounding in my ears, I drew in more of her web, but I was running out of time.

Breaking the strand off, I scanned the branches above. I ignored her hisses as I climbed, moving toward a limb stretching closer to the final platform. Perched there, I studied the branches extending out from the other tree and when I'd selected the right one, I broke off a chunk of branch and secured it to the end of the web.

The tree twitched above me, and a glance up showed the spider had used her web to fly from the other tree to this one.

She clung to the trunk, peering down.

Then she started crawling toward me.

CHAPTER 33

LYNETH

I stood with about twenty orcs, watching as the three males made their way through the challenges. Fretting, I kept biting my tongue to keep from crying out. The rest, other than perhaps Dakur, watched raptly yet dispassionately.

Dakur kept shooting me concerned glances. Did he hope Madr would win, or did he just pray Madr wasn't devoured by the spider? I assumed hearing that a male from the Lumen Clan had died while under their care, so to speak, would not reflect well.

Madr continued to coil up the spider web, and I couldn't imagine what he hoped to do with it.

Meanwhile, Pulost lay across the black pool below, slowly making his way across the thick, gooey surface. Bubbles periodically rose to the top and burst, shooting sparks and spores into the air. It stunk all the way up here on the platform. It must reek horribly on his level.

Still, he was at least a quarter of the way across the swamp.

Finsteg had climbed up onto a precariously thin branch and was studying the gap between there and the upper branches of the enormous tree where we waited. The trunk behind me might be many arms' lengths around, but some of the upper limbs couldn't be wider than my wrist. Even if they'd support his weight, that didn't mean he could jump from there to the top of this tree. The distance appeared too vast to me.

The spider crept closer to Madr as he worked feverishly, attaching a piece of wood to the end of the web.

"How does he plan to cross?" Sessavia whispered beside me.

Dakur nodded slowly. "Clever."

"What's he doing?" I asked.

This was no longer about one of them winning and claiming me. I just wanted Madr to survive. If the spider got him . . . No, I didn't want to think about that.

My eyes stung with tears, and I brushed them off my cheeks. I needed to hold strong and believe he'd survive.

"We won't allow him to die," Dakur said softly, his gaze meeting mine. "We treasure each other too much to waste a life, which means none of the competitors will perish during this challenge. But if any of them needs help . . ." He shrugged. "They lose unless they can complete this on their own using their own abilities and ingenuity. But their final fate will not be decided today."

Somehow, that didn't relieve me one bit.

I hovered near the edge of the platform, clinging to the rail that was at chest-level for me and waist-height for an orc.

My lungs were on fire from breathing fast, and my heart was a furious drum in my chest.

Madr finished what he was doing with the end of the web, shooting worried looks at the spider who continued to creep down the trunk toward him.

"She's going to grab him," I gulped out. "Save him. I'll accept whatever you make me do after that."

"It's not over yet," Dakur said, lifting his arm. One of the other males leaped and grabbed onto a branch above. He'd coiled a long vine around his waist that he slowly unwound. When it dangled, with the end tied to his loin-cloth, he flung his arm out and the vine soared up and toward the other tree. It flipped around a branch high above Madr. The male crouched and poised to swing in Madr's direction.

Pulost had made it to the middle of the pool and was still floundering in our direction. More bubbles rose around him, and then the murky stuff he swam through started churning.

Dakur nodded to another male waiting on the plat-form, and this one swung a vine up to secure it to a branch overhead like the first. He, too, waited to swing down and snatch Pulost from the muck if he found himself in trouble.

When the water erupted beside Pulost, he flailed, struggling to go faster. A large, black blob with a single eye emerged near him and tentacled limbs snapped out from beneath the surface, wrapping around Pulost.

He bellowed and smacked the limbs. They snapped away, and the inky beast released a high-pitched shriek that echoed around us. More limbs flicked out, coiling around Pulost again. He screamed and tried to wrench away.

Dakur blew across his pendant, creating a low musical hum. Pulost looked up with stark fear cratering his face.

"Yes?" Dakur asked.

Pulost jerked out a nod, and the male waiting swung down on the vine toward Pulost, a sword in his hand. He swiped the blunted end across the creature as he passed, and it released Pulost, sinking back down into the thick pool.

On his return swing, the male stretched an arm toward Pulost, and he grabbed it.

Others on the platform then pulled them up, and in a short time, Pulost stood near Dakur, dripping black goo onto the platform.

He sent me a forlorn look and clutched his pendant that no longer glowed.

Madr eased himself farther out onto a branch as the spider reached the very limb he lay on and started crawling along it in his direction.

He jumped to his feet and coiled the end of the webbing around his wrist. His gaze met mine, and I swore I read excitement, not fear there.

Finsteg cried out in terror, and I whipped my head in that direction, finding him clinging to the very tip of a vine, dangling over the swampy water.

"Yes?" Dakur called out, and Finsteg nodded.

A male swung down toward him, grabbing Finsteg around the waist as he passed, and they continued together toward the tree Finsteg had attempted to swing from. They landed squarely on a branch before jumping off again and flying in this direction. When they reached us, his pendant's light winked out.

He nodded in my direction and strode across the decking to the trunk of the tree. A metal platform soon projected him toward a nearby tree, and in no time, he'd disappeared into the foliage.

"If Madr can reach us, he has won," Dakur said with satisfaction.

A soft sound sent me spinning.

The spider reared back, lifting her claws to drive them into Madr's back.

He leaped off the branch and plunged toward the ground.

CHAPTER 34

MADR

Gathering all my strength and holding tight to the thick strand of web, I launched myself into the broad, empty gap between the tree I stood on and my destination.

Lyneth watched, and all I wanted to do was stop and stare at her. She was infinite beauty, my hope and my blessing.

But I didn't have time.

That was the problem with life. There was *never* enough time.

The air rushed past me as I reached the end of the web with a snap. It held, thank the fates, and my momentum carried me toward the other tree. Had I gauged the distance and trajectory enough to make this work?

Would the webbing give way?

I wanted to close my eyes and let this happen as the

fates willed, but if I'd learned nothing else while growing up with distant family members trying to kill me to take my place in line for the throne, I knew it was best to face what came at you with your eyes wide open.

For one terrifying moment, time seemed to slow. Everything blurred into a whirlwind of purple foliage passing by at breakneck speed. My grip tightened on the hilardep web wrapped around my wrist.

The distance closed rapidly as I swung toward the platform where everyone waited.

My pace slowed.

I wasn't going to make it.

The lavender forest rushed beneath me, streaked with veins of golden sunlight. My nostrils filled with a mix scents. The damp musky aroma of the swamp below and a floral scent drifting from blossoms.

Behind me, the hilardep female shrieked in anger. Would she follow?

I peered back to see her poised on the edge of the branch I'd left, peering up. She spit out a strand of webbing and it snagged on the very branch I swung from. A leap, and she rushed toward me.

When I smacked hard into something, I yanked my attention away from her and clung to the trunk a few arms' lengths below the platform.

I unwound the web from my hand and released it, then started to climb using the sides of my feet to hold my balance.

Dakur blew across his pendant; I recognized the

sound, and males swung down on vines to dangle nearby.

"Do you need help?" one asked solemnly. "Know that having help before you finish the course means defeat." His gaze shot to the spider. "She is close."

Not close enough.

"The other two have lost," I growled, climbing as fast as I could.

He dipped his head forward.

"Don't help me."

The spider landed lightly on the tree trunk below me, and with murder in her four eyes, she began scrambling up the tree in my direction.

I climbed as quickly as I could, the distance narrowing much too slowly.

Time almost seemed suspended as my horns bumped into the platform above me. I reached out with desperate fingers to grasp onto the wooden edge.

With a grunt, I hauled myself up through a small opening and onto the landing, yanking my legs up before she could grab them. My breath came in ragged gasps as my heart thumped against ribcage like a beast seeking escape through flesh and bone.

Shrieks rang out below, telling me how angry she was that I'd escaped.

The hatch closed and her shrieks faded. They were driving her away.

I rose to my shaky feet.

I'd finished the course. I'd triumphed over the others. And now it was time to claim my mate for the final time.

CHAPTER 35
LYNETH

When Madr rose to his feet, a big grin on his tired face, I flung myself at him, clinging. He was safe and that was all that mattered.

To think I'd wanted to run from him not long ago. Now I couldn't imagine a future without him.

I linked my arm with his as Dakur strode over to us.

He braced Madr's shoulders. "Well done, friend. Well done. It was close there for a moment."

"The hilardep spider was an unexpected surprise." Madr looked down at me, his eyes so full of heat, it stole the wind from my lungs. His pendant flared brighter than a shooting star. "Now I'd like to be alone with my mate."

"I'm sure you would." Dakur released a low chuckle. "But we must celebrate first. You've waited this long, what's a bit more time?"

Madr growled and his body tightened, his muscles

bunching as if he would scoop me up and leap off the platform, racing into the forest. With a grunt, he softened, shaking his head.

"Only a *short* time." His hand slid down my arm to clasp my fingers. "We'll briefly join your celebration, and then, we'll leave."

He must be exhausted from what he'd just been through, yet he appeared as unruffled as he'd been at the start.

Dakur blew across his pendant, and a different sound rang out, this one light and musical. How did he do it?

Another similar sound echoed in the forest. It was repeated in a sequence, as if one orc after another blew across their pendants to send the message forward.

A whipping sound made me catch my breath, and a series of vines snapped out from a tree some distance behind us. The vines landed on this platform and wove into the platform. In no time, a new bridge had been formed.

"Your clan pendants can speak to the vines?" Madr asked in amazement.

Dakur dipped his head forward. "We don't share secrets."

"You already did."

Dakur's laugh rang out. "Perhaps I did and perhaps I didn't. Come." He strode over to the bridge and started across it.

We followed. Whenever we reached a new platform, more vines would whip out to join us to another tree.

Not long after, we'd moved far beyond where Madr had struggled hard to complete the course.

My pulse had slowed to a more normal rhythm, and my curiosity had been sparked. Where were they taking us?

We finally reached the biggest platform I'd seen so far; one constructed all the way around an enormous tree. A railing circled the outer part of the smooth surface, and many orcs had gathered there already. The smell of roasted meat and the sound of music filled the air.

"Tonight, we celebrate," Dakur said, stopping before he reached the platform. "It's rare for a clan pendant to choose a mate, and even rarer for multiple pendants to do so. I can barely remember the last time three males had to compete for the opportunity to claim a female. We've prepared a meal, and we'd be honored if you shared it with us. After, we've arranged for a place where you can sleep. Once you've rested, we'll take you back to your vox who will be loaded with provisions for the rest of your journey."

I grinned up at Madr. "We can stay for a meal, right?"

He nodded. "Then we'll leave."

I was eager to be alone with him, to show him how much he'd come to mean to me.

For the first time, I was eager to give my body to someone. Knowing he'd be mine fully before morning made heat coast through my veins.

"Please, you're our guests," Dakur said, reaching the

platform and gesturing to tables nearby, one placed near the tree trunk with three seats. "Sit with me, and we'll be served."

I sunk down next to Madr with Dakur on his other side. In no time, orcs placed platters overloaded with food in front of us, enough to feed a good portion of my village.

"Do they always eat like this?" I whispered to Madr.

He shrugged.

"We're a simple people," Dakur said, leaning around Madr to speak to me. "Normally, we prepare our meals in our homes and eat there. But tonight, we have you two with us." His eyes sparkled. "It's not often we have guests."

"I don't believe other orc clans ever visit yours, do they?" Madr asked, his steely gaze on Dakur.

"While it's true we've never invited your king or anyone from your clan here, you're wrong if you think you're our first guest."

"Who visits the Matis Clan?"

"Now that's an amazing question." Dakur nudged a platter full of meat toward me. "Please. Would you like me to serve you, or would you prefer to do so yourself?"

Shaking my head, I selected a few cuts of meat and put them on my plate, adding bread, vegetables, and fruit unlike anything I'd seen before. Was it grown here in the forest, or did they trade for things such as this with the mythical people he suggested visit?

Madr and Dakur also took food, eating quickly. We

washed it down with a slightly sweet drink that was surprisingly refreshing. It also made my pulse thud faster. I kept resisting the urge to giggle.

"Is this alcohol?" Madr asked, lifting his mug and frowning at the contents.

"Fillawate is made from a very rare fruit that grows deep beneath the ground," Dakur said. "We pick it in the fall and make the brew, but it's not fermented, so no alcohol. The fruit itself contains properties that make the person drinking it feel happy. And who doesn't want something like that?" He lifted his mug and we tapped ours against his.

I took another sip but decided to be cautious. I loved the giddy feeling it gave me, but I wanted to keep my wits about me. This place was dangerous, as the spider already proved.

And was it right to slide into Madr's bed if this drink could partly drive my actions? Although, I'd already decided it was time. I wanted to be with him. It felt like it had been weeks since we'd kissed, or he'd touched me.

I needed more.

As we were finishing our meals, a few orcs got up and started dancing, their plodding feet making loud thuds on the wooden platform. They held up their mugs and twirled together. I noted how few females were here.

"The rest of your women," I said above the furor, "are they elsewhere tonight?"

"Sadly, no. My clan is made up of almost five hundred orcs, but only twenty are female."

"Why?"

"In the orc city where I come from," Madr said, "the shaydes attacked, killing many of our females."

"That didn't happen here," Dakur said. "No, instead, we've seen a decline in the birth of orclings overall and the majority of those born are male. Tenkaril insists change is coming, that things will improve, but I'm not sure how it can." He frowned and studied his partly eaten meal. "She said I must go on a journey, that it will be fraught with danger. That there is a chance I'll find my true mate and bond with her. Then things will get better for our clan. I'm not sure how me mating with someone could make a difference. One couple cannot replenish our clan."

"Your clan hasn't participated in the hunt," Madr said.

Dakur shrugged. "We didn't enter the treaty with the other clans."

"Why not? It's a chance to find a mate." Beneath the table, Madr took my hand and squeezed it. "If my clan didn't participate, I never would've found Lyneth."

"I'd like to think the fates will gift me with a mate whether I participate in a hunt or not," Dakur said. "Or a journey, for that matter."

"None in your clan have sparked your pendant?" Madr asked.

Dakur shook his head. "Perhaps I need to take this journey Tenkaril refers to. Then I'll make it happen." He shot me a sad smile. "I'd like to find someone I can treasure always. Wouldn't everyone?"

That was exactly how I felt. I'd found that person in Madr.

As if on cue, Tenkaril melted away from the enormous tree trunk. With help, she came over to stand in front of us. Her smile fell on me. "You've made a wise choice."

There never was a choice, was there? Madr had always been mine, and I belonged to him. But instead of stating this, I just nodded.

Tenkaril turned to Madr. "You, I must also see."

He glanced my way and cleared his throat. "All right."

Did he understand her ways? He must, because he held still while she placed her hands on his face and ran her thumbs across his closed eyelids.

"Hmm," she said. "Interesting."

"What do you see?" he asked, shooting me a look I couldn't define.

"Not enough and too much." Her cackle rang out. "But I strive to never be vague. All I can say is that time is important, and it moves much too slowly."

"*That* is vague."

She tapped his shoulder. "Don't be impertinent."

He bowed his head. "I apologize."

"When the time is right, you'll know what you must do," she added.

"All right."

With that, she turned and strode over to Dakur

who'd risen and was speaking with some of the males. When she crooked her finger his way, he bent closer, and she "saw" him as well, but we didn't hear what she told him.

He nodded and kissed her cheek.

Tenkaril patted his arm "Be well, my son."

Ah, she was his mother? Interesting.

"You as well, adopted son," she told Zickar.

He kissed her cheek.

She left the group, clinging to her assistant's arm as she stepped onto a bridge leading to a tree quite some distance away.

I gave Madr a raised-brow look, and he shrugged.

When night fell, the dancing slowed, and some of the orcs returned to tables where they played games on the wooden surfaces. Musicians created softer tunes, and a few orc families left.

"We probably should go as well," Madr said, his gaze shooting to me.

"Of course. I'd never hold you here," Dakur said. "However, we're still happy to offer you a place to sleep. You could depart in the morning."

Madr turned to me. "What say you, mate? Should we leave now or remain here and . . . rest?"

I squeezed his hand. "Let's take Dakur up on his offer and rest."

CHAPTER 36

MADR

Lyneth looked at me with so much affection, it made my heart ache.

I wanted to be with her more than anything. Our first time should be special, not while lying on the ground where I'd have to worry about creatures attacking, let alone the surface we're we'd finally be together.

A soft bed would be most welcome.

Standing, I swept her up and kissed her. She tasted even sweeter than the fillawate. The way she wrapped her arms around me and the way she pressed herself against me made me want to hold her forever. Love her for always.

Someone cheered and others joined in. I wasn't embarrassed that they knew what we'd soon do. They were happy for us, happy to see a true mated couple. Each and every one of them no doubt hoped they'd be in this position themselves one day as well.

"Where?" I asked Dakur when I lifted my head.

Lyneth hid her face in my neck. My lovely mate wasn't used to everyone knowing we were about to have sex, but orcs were more relaxed about this. She'd soon see she had nothing to be concerned about.

"Follow me," Dakur said, blowing across his pendant. A vine bridge snapped down from above to connect this tree to another we hadn't been to so far, though I couldn't be completely sure. My sense of direction was good, but they were more at home in the canopy than me.

He strode across it, and I followed, carrying Lyneth in my arms. At the next tree, he proceeded across a second bridge. Three more followed, and with each, we drew farther away from the music and the sound of orcs dancing and playing boisterous games. If I had my guess, they'd celebrate until dawn. We'd find them nursing headaches and with blurry eyes in the morning.

Finally, Dakur came to a stop on a small platform perched higher in the trees than most of the others. A small building had been built close to the tree itself, and when he opened the door, the interior extended well into the enormous trunk.

Polished wooden walls with small windows looked out at the forest on two sides.

A tub big enough for two orcs had been placed in the corner, and steam coiled off the lavender water. An enormous bed dominated the room, and fresh clothing had been draped across the back of a big chair in the corner.

Pitchers and a tray had been left on a narrow table, and I assumed the pitchers held water or more of the potent brew they adored, fillawate.

"I'll see you in the morning?" Dakur asked, backing from the room with pure envy gleaming in his eyes. He might say he was in no rush to mate, but I suspected he was lonely. This was the way of things when the person had no choice but to rule.

Perhaps he'd reconsider and go to the hunt next year. Despite not signing the treaty, he'd be welcome.

As the door swung closed, I pushed all thought of my friend from my mind.

Now was for me and Lyneth, and I wasn't going to waste a moment.

CHAPTER 37

LYNETH

Madr placed me on my feet but remained close, staring down at me.

"Never feel pressured, sweet one," he said in a gravelly tone that tickled across my bones.

"I could say the same, mate."

"There isn't anything I want more in life than to love you, please you."

Thanks to him, I knew enough about my body now to know that only bliss would come from what we'd do next. In some ways, I felt as if I was still a maiden, wondering about what went on in the bedroom. But Madr had shown me that I not only had nothing to fear, but that there was joy to be found in what a mated couple did together.

"Then why are we standing here?" I shot him a sultry smile. I lifted my dress up over my head and tossed it aside. The orcs hadn't provided me with any undergarments. I'd left mine to be washed with the rest of my clothing.

Madr gazed at me with so much heat in his eyes, my skin practically smoldered. I couldn't wait to feel everything with him.

I sauntered around him, tracing my finger across his waist and lower spine. "I believe we should climb into the tub before the water gets cold, don't you, love?"

"Lyneth," he groaned. "I want you so much."

The stiff cock beneath his loincloth proved his words.

With another smile, I walked over to the tub and climbed inside, settling with a groan in the hot water.

"Your muscles must be sore," I said. "Watching you complete the challenges both terrified and amazed me."

He unwound his loincloth tie. "How much did you see?"

"All of it. Dakur kept blowing across his pendant and vine bridges would appear. Some went nowhere other than closer to the course. He'd lead me to the end, which was both scary and wondrous since I couldn't see how they remained suspended. We'd watch from there as you made your way through each challenge. I swear, they use magic in this clan."

"I can't imagine such a thing is possible." But then I thought of Tenkaril's words. Could her prophecy be trusted or was it just the mutterings of an elderly orc? I'd share it with Madr tomorrow when we traveled.

Tonight was for focusing on being with my mate.

Madr tossed the loincloth aside and strode toward

me, his cock big and thick, thrusting against his taut belly. He stopped beside the tub and stared down at me. "You're so tiny and delicate."

"I'm tougher than I look."

"I never want to hurt you."

"I assume there will be times when you won't be able to help it. Know I'll always forgive you."

"I also meant me somehow stuffing this," he tapped his cock with a bead of precum on the tip, "inside your tight little passage."

"My tight little passage is getting wet. I ache to feel you inside me. You know I didn't find pleasure in the act before. Can you show me how wonderful it can be?"

With a heady groan, he climbed into the tub and settled across from me, taking my hand and tugging me onto his lap.

"I suppose we should bathe," I said with a laugh as his fingertips traced down my chest and latched onto my nipples. "Or not."

"Not," he whispered, leaning forward to kiss my ear, suck on the lobe, then trailing his lips along my jawline. "Definitely not."

He kissed me, and it was sweet and loving. My pulse soared through the roof, and I pressed myself against him while his hands slid down my sides. He spread my legs and seated me on his lap, his cock thrusting up between us. I rubbed against it, eager to know what it would feel like moving inside me.

My bones melted as his tongue glided across mine.

He traced his fingers between my legs, where he stroked my clit.

I moaned and thrust against him, marveling at how little he had to touch me to make everything inside me burst into flames.

He slid a finger inside me, and I tipped my head back and rode it. Was that wanton of me? Absolutely. But I trusted Madr to make this night special, to give me what no one else had before.

He growled as he watched me. "You're beautiful. So responsive. I love how you take what you need."

"I crave your touch, mate. You." With a whimper, I lifted and dropped on his finger. His thumb glided across my clit, and this was pure bliss. I wasn't sure I could hold out any longer, but I needed to feel his big cock deep inside me. I'd been missing out on something wonderful, and it was past time I found it.

"Would you like to ride me instead of my finger?" he asked, his tusks grazing the skin of my neck.

Lifting up, I slid off his fingers and latched onto his cock.

Then I placed it at my opening and dropped onto it.

I was going to explode before I was seated deeply inside her.

"You feel amazing," I said. "So perfect."

She growled and lifted her body, pushing down onto me again, but we weren't making much progress.

"How can we get it inside?" she whimpered.

I shouldn't laugh but I felt so happy, I couldn't help it.

Freezing, she glared down at me. "You either help me out here or . . ." She huffed. "Or I don't know what I'm going to do."

I eased her off the tip of my cock and climbed out of the tub with her in my arms. Laying her on the bed, I flipped her on to belly and lifted her hips, centering the head of my cock at her core. "Let's try it this way, sweet one."

I gripped her hips tightly, my fingers digging into her

flesh as I slowly pushed inside her. She gasped and moaned beneath me, her fingers gripping the sheets as her body quivered.

"You feel wonderful," she said into the pillow. "Don't stop."

"It's nowhere near over yet, love." Pulling out, I pushed back in, groaning at how incredible her body felt sliding around and squeezing my cock. I started moving, taking a slow, steady pace at first, giving her body time to adjust to mine.

Soon, the room was filled with the sound of our heavy breathing and the slick, erotic shift of our bodies moving together. When she started moaning and pushing back to meet me, I went faster, thrusting deep and hard into her. Her moans grew louder, and I could feel her body tightening around mine.

My cock quivered, showing how into this I was. My mate consumed my every thought, and all I could think of was how much I cared for her, how important it was to me that she found pleasure in this.

Her back arched, and she pressed her breasts firmly against the bed as she met each of my drives. Heat built between us, tightening and coiling with every delicious thrust. The scent of our desire hung in the air, mingling with the sounds of our passion. My spur rotated and latched onto her clit, sucking it, and her shriek of pleasure lit up the night.

I leaned forward, my hands gripping her hips even

tighter, and whispered into her ear. "You feel so good. You're tight and wet for me, and I adore you."

She whimpered, her body jerking back to meet mine. "I need something, Madr. Please."

"I'm going to give you everything, mate. All I have to give." I was hers already. I would be until my dying day.

Holding her hips, I increased the speed and force of my thrusts, plunging into her with an almost feral hunger. Waves of heat crashed over me, and it was all I could do not to explode inside her.

She cried out as her orgasm washed over her, her nails raking across the sheets. Her body convulsed beneath me, the walls of her core squeezing me, pushing me closer to the edge.

With one final drive, I held myself deep within her as my own release crashed through me, my entire being consumed by the joy of being with my mate. My shout echoed in the room.

Groaning her name, I collapsed onto the bed beside her, our bodies slick with water from the bath and still locked together.

We lay together as our breathing slowly returned to normal.

I shifted her around until she lay across my chest and gave her a gentle smile. "Good?"

"Madr," she sighed. "It was . . ." Tears filled her eyes.

Terrified I'd done something wrong; I tightened my arms around her. "You're all right? I didn't hurt you?"

She grinned through her tears. "I think the only thing that'll hurt me is if you don't do it again."

In no time, we were all over each other again.

After she'd ridden me, we bathed, then fed each other from a tray placed on a low table.

We returned to bed, and I made love to her from the front.

Finally, we fell asleep wrapped in each other's arms.

We woke to someone banging on the door.

I sat up, giving Lyneth a concerned look. I slipped from the bed and strode to the door naked, opening the panel. "Dakur."

He thrust his way inside, turning away when he caught sight of Lyneth lying on the bed, though she was completely covered. "I'm sorry. I would never disturb you unless I had to."

"What's wrong?" I shot my mate another worried look.

"Your brother reached out to all the clans."

"Jaus? Why?" I asked, wrapping a drying cloth around his waist.

"It's your father. He's had some kind of spell. He can't speak or move his left side and . . ." Dakur gripped my shoulders and the sympathy in his gaze was like a spear through the chest. "He's not expected to survive. That's not all, however." A snarl ripped from his throat. "Your cousin, Riank, is claiming he has the right to the throne."

"Throne?" I asked Madr, confused. "What's Dakur talking about?"

"I . . ." He wrenched his gaze from mine, turning it toward the wooden floorboards. "I abdicated. I was angry with my father for scorning my half-brother Jaus, and I told him I no longer wanted to be a part of his life."

I climbed out of bed, pulling a blanket along with me to keep my body covered. "Please tell me what this is all about."

Dakur looked between us. "I assume you'll wish to leave as soon as possible?"

Madr nodded.

"I'll have someone pack enough food and water for your journey." He hissed something I didn't understand. "And that's not all. Jaus also relayed that Riank's younger brother was with him at your father's side, but only for a brief time. Jaus believes Riank sent his younger brother to make sure you don't reach the orc kingdom before it's too late."

Raking his fingers through his hair, Madr swore. "I need to get to the kingdom."

"You'll take the throne if something happens to your father?" Dakur asked.

"I don't know what I'll do," Madr snarled. "But I need to get there yesterday."

"Very well." Dakur nodded slowly. "I'm sorry about your father."

Madr braced Dakur's shoulders. "Thank you, friend. For everything."

Dakur left, shutting the door softly behind him.

"What does that mean, that Riank sent his brother after you?" I asked.

"It means we'll have to be very careful while flying to the kingdom."

My breath caught. "He'd harm us?"

"Riank will do almost anything to claim the throne." Madr turned to me and, taking my hand, tugged me over to the chair. He sat and pulled me onto his lap, his arms going around me. He rested his chin on the top of my head. "I used to be the heir to the orc kingdom."

"*Used* to be?" I wasn't sure why I focused on that and not the fact that he'd just told me he was . . . Wow. A prince.

"I'm sorry," he said. "I didn't share everything about myself with you, when I should've from the start."

I hadn't either. Was now the time?

"Tell me," I said. Once he'd finished, it would be my turn.

"My father is the orc king. Some might say he rules over all the clans, though I don't believe Dakur would agree. King Thourand considers me his only son, but that's not true. Jaus is my half-brother. He was born two years before me, and I love him. I hate that my father scorns him, that he allows others to mock him. And I hate that he hasn't acknowledged Jaus as his eldest son and true heir. He has a granddaughter he hasn't seen once, and that's his fault. Jaus reached out after she was born, probably feeling he must, but my father didn't reply to the message."

"That's cruel." I couldn't wait to see my sister, to snuggle my niece. I'd adore her as much as Madr.

I was stunned to think her grandfather wanted nothing to do with her or her father. Madr had mentioned it recently, but I still couldn't believe he and Rhoslyn's mate were half-brothers. The fates worked in mysterious ways.

"Almost a year ago, Rhoslyn was injured. She recovered at the seaside palace, tended by the best healers in the kingdom. That was my father's chance to proclaim Jaus as his son and heir, his chance to welcome his new daughter into his life. Everyone would've rejoiced. Instead, he scorned Jaus once more, plus Rhoslyn."

"He sounds . . ." I wanted to say *horrible*. To rail about how mean and unkind he had been to my sister and Jaus, but this was Madr's father. His feelings must be incredibly conflicted. "That sounds unfair."

"He's an ass. I told him so. And I told him I was done with him." His rueful laugh echoed in the room. "I told him I abdicated the throne, that he could do whatever he wanted with it. I moved to my mother's childhood home and ignored him after that. It wasn't until a few days before the hunt that I saw him. He came to me and tried to talk me into stepping back into my role in the kingdom."

"What did you say?"

"That I didn't want to be king. Truly, I don't. Jaus would make a much better king. I don't have the will to do what must be done, but as the commander of our military, Jaus does."

"So you left for the hunt at an impasse."

"There was nothing else I could do. He insisted I must take the throne after he was gone, and I insisted I didn't want that role."

"It sounds like your cousin will take it then." Although, I suspected after he'd fought Madr, and then stabbed Brakkis, Riank would be a harsh and unjust king. But maybe that was what the kingdom needed since it sounded as if Madr's father held the same tendencies.

"Even worse," Madr said. "Before I left, my father tried to talk me out of participating in the hunt. He's . . . he feels humans aren't good enough for orcs."

"I'm sorry. I'm sure that was hurtful."

"I don't feel the same way at all. We're all people. None of us are better than any other. I love you, Lyneth, and that's what matters most."

I turned on his lap and hugged him. "I love you too, Madr."

"My sweet mate," he growled and kissed me. He cupped my face and stared into my eyes. "No matter what, we'll be together. Know that."

"We need to leave. You father's sick, and he needs you."

He snorted, but his eyes remained somber. "I'm not convinced he needs anyone but himself, but you're right. We need to leave. He's stricken with sickness, and it's my place as his son to be with him during this time."

"What will you do about your cousin?"

His steely gaze met mine. "I can't let my cousin take the throne."

"But you don't want it yourself. Would you relent and take it if that was the only option?"

"I don't know." He sighed. "I'm not the right person to rule."

"And your cousin? Maybe he'll do a decent job once he's settled into the role."

"He only thinks of himself. He'd be a worse ruler than me."

"I imagine you'll figure this out before we get there." I couldn't maintain a connection with his eyes, so I focused on his chest, stroking it while I stared blindly. "I haven't been completely honest either."

"What do you mean?" He lifted my chin.

I could wrench my gaze away. He'd never force me to do anything I wasn't comfortable with, but it would be wrong not just to withhold this from him but to look away while I told him. "My sister is Rhoslyn."

He frowned, and his head tilted as he studied my face. "I see some resemblance now that you tell me. Why didn't you mention it earlier?"

"In all honesty, when I left the village, I was determined to use you."

His thick brow lifted. "How did you plan to do that?"

"Not *you* specifically, just whoever claimed me in the hunt. I planned to urge whoever that was to take me near to where she lives. After that, I planned to escape, run to her, and beg her to give me sanctuary."

"And what do you plan to do now?"

"Stay with you. Love you. And visit my sister when I can."

His eyes sparkled. Wasn't he angry with me for holding this back?

"No begging for sanctuary?" he asked.

"You're all the protection I need. No, you're *all* I need. My plan applied to an unknown orc." Because he didn't appear upset about this, my tension eased, and I sent him a relieved smile. "You're not mad at me."

"Why would I be? If you told me you still planned to

run, I'd be sad. Devastated, actually, but you must know I'd never hold you back if that was what you wanted."

"Thank you, for claiming me and for understanding."

"I love you, Lyneth. I doubt there's anything you could do that would ever change that."

"Then I hope that day never comes."

CHAPTER 40

MADR

We washed quickly and dressed in the clothing provided. Zickar waited for us outside the door, and I introduced him to Lyneth.

"Here are your cleaned things, plus food and water." He handed me two bags that I flung over my shoulder. They banged against my flail sheathed on my spine. Dakur had been confident we'd stay the night and left it there for me.

I dipped my head toward Zickar. "Thank you."

"Dakur went ahead to make sure Brakkis has fully healed."

"That's kind of him," I said.

"Alone," Zickar growled.

"Are you concerned something could harm him?" Lyneth asked, frowning at Zickar.

He shook his head, but that wasn't exactly an

answer. He lifted his pendant and blew across it, generating a subtly different sound than the one Dakur made last night to control the vines. This time, instead of vines snapping out to create a bridge, a platform shot up from the ground, coming to a stop beside us.

He nodded for us to step onto it, and the three of us were quickly taken to the ground.

"How do you make these?" I asked. "They're metal, and I haven't seen any indication you have blacksmiths or metalworkers, let alone a shop. And how do they work?"

Zickar grunted but that also wasn't an answer.

"More secrets?" I asked.

Zickar shot us a sly grin. "Always."

We followed him through the woods, weaving around enormous trees. I was a decent tracker, but even I was soon lost. Only hearing the soft murmur of voices overhead told me we were still within the clan's boundaries. But there were few direct trails; they must use vine bridges to travel almost everywhere.

"Do you fly with voxes?" I asked Zickar in a low voice, not interested in drawing the attention of shaydes or other dangerous creatures. "I haven't seen any." Of course, theirs could nest a distance away like ours often did. They had acute hearing and always remained within shouting distance of their bonded orc.

"Why would we need to fly on a creature when we can travel through the canopy with leaps or vine bridges?" he asked.

"You might one day wish to travel beyond the forest or across the ground."

"When we do, we travel in a different way."

"You run?" I frowned, wondering what he could mean. "I haven't heard of the Matis Clan traveling beyond the forest."

"We don't announce it to the world, but we've ventured even to the edge of the desert landscape occupied by the Ember Clan where the rest of you bond with vox young after they slip from their seed."

"What's beyond the Ember lands? I've never traveled there."

Zickar grinned again.

I huffed. "Still more secrets?"

He put his arm around my shoulder as we walked side by side with Lyneth holding my other hand. "One day, perhaps you will be worthy."

"This is because I wasn't born Matis."

He slipped away and strode ahead of us. "One doesn't always need our blood churning through their veins to claim our clan as their own."

I suspected I was going to be forced into a position that would never allow me to claim anything but the Lumen Clan. I loved my people. There wasn't much I wouldn't do for them, but that might mean taking the throne solely to keep my cousin from claiming it. This wasn't a power struggle between me and my cousin, more me admitting that despite not wishing to wear the crown, I'd probably do a better job while wearing it than he could ever dream of.

It was funny how the idea of stepping back into the position I'd scorned didn't bother me as much as it had in the past. Perhaps I was unsettled because it sounded as if my father was dying. I'd always seen him as the strength in the family, the rock. It was hard to believe he could be dead before I reached the city.

We continued to follow Zickar, leaving the hushed sound of orcs moving above and behind us.

But when we left the slight path and stepped out into the meadow, Dakur wasn't waiting.

Neither was my vox, Brakkis.

CHAPTER 41

LYNETH

I leaned close to Madr and spoke softly. "Where are they?"

"No idea." He tightened his fingers on his staff and stepped away from me, peering around. Releasing a low hum from deep in his throat, he waited, his head cocked as if he listened.

When it was clear Brakkis wouldn't—our couldn't—respond to his call, Madr growled.

Zickar had backed up to the edge of the woods. He studied the vegetation with swords in both hands. Finally, his posture loosened. "Gone." Sheathing his swords at his waist, he jogged into the clearing and stooped down in the area where I remember seeing Brakkis last.

He ran his fingers along the ground as Madr and I approached him. "Still warm," he whispered. "Blood. Too much."

"From Brakkis?" I asked.

"It's green. Orc." Zickar stood, fury bristling on his face. He strode around in widening circles, studying the ground before lifting his pendant and blowing across it.

No sound came from the gesture.

We waited in silence until the thunder of heavy paws rushing this way made me scoot closer to Madr. My spine tingled with fear, and I whipped my head around, wondering what was going to happen next.

Three shaydes bolted into the clearing. Madr urged me behind him, lifting his staff and growling.

The shaydes came to a halt not far away, but instead of baring their fangs or leaping on us, claws extended, they stared at Zickar.

He blew across his pendant again, this time making a medium-pitched sound, and two orcs melted out of the vegetation behind him.

"Someone has taken our caedos," Zickar said grimly. "I'm going after him."

"But you're second-in-command," one of the two other males said. "You need to remain here."

"One of you will travel with me," Zickar said, ignoring the comments. "We'll leave as soon as possible, and we'll travel lightly."

The males grunted and rushed back into the woods, ignoring the shaydes that stared at us with hungry eyes.

Tenkaril slipped from the woods with her helper. She strode over to Zickar and held up her hands, grunting. He bent forward and she "saw" him, stepping back quickly.

"When you find them, it's vital you listen," she said. Pivoting, she strode back into the woods.

My entire world was upside down.

My skin was on fire with fear, and I wanted to flee, but I knew the shaydes would take me down within seconds and rip me apart.

"I'm sorry, but I need to leave," Zickar said to us, fear darkening his eyes.

Madr watched the shaydes. "I don't understand any of this."

"Someone has harmed Dakur. They took him from the meadow, and I suspect they either stole or frightened away your vox."

"If they killed either of them, their bodies would still be here. Brakkis isn't responding to my call," Madr said, scanning the skies. "He wouldn't leave me, and he would come to my call if he could."

Zickar strode closer to one of the shaydes, and I braced myself for it to attack. I'd stepped into the middle of a nightmare, and nothing made sense. "Your cousin appears determined to make sure you never make it to the orc kingdom."

Madr grunted, still glaring at the shaydes. "He'll do all he can to keep me from arriving in the city before it's too late to stop him from claiming the throne. If my father dies, the elders will meet and choose a new king. Since I abdicated the throne, it won't be me."

"Why are we standing here while shaydes appear

ready to make us their next meal?" I asked shrilly. It wasn't that I was unsympathetic to what was happening with Dakur and Brakkis, but the shaydes were an immediate threat.

"They won't attack," Zickar said in a low, soothing tone. "Will you?" He actually reached out and stroked the head of the nearest shayde, who leaned into his touch, closed its eyes, and . . . purred?

"This isn't possible," I hissed.

"And yet it is." Zickar stood in front of a shayde and whispered. The creature nudged his belly, and Zickar released a dry laugh. "You're wise to fear them, but three years ago, Dakur came across a nest of shayde kits. Rather than kill them, he brought them back here. Each of us claimed one and raised them like one would pets. While they returned to the wild once they'd grown, they've remained friendly to all in our clan. In fact, *they* are now clan, as loved and protected as even our most treasured elder." He sent me and Madr a worried look. "If anyone can find Dakur's scent and follow it, it will be them."

One of the orc males he'd called returned with a pack strapped to his back. He handed a second to Zickar.

"I have to look for Brakkis, but I don't know where to start," Madr said, peering at the sky.

"I suspect if you ask your cousin, he may have an answer." Zickar gestured to the shayde he'd been patting. "Millamay will take you as close to the orc kingdom as she can. You can leave her after that, and she'll return to us."

"It's a long journey," Madr said.

Frankly, that was the last thing I thought about. How were we supposed to travel with a beast who'd kill us if it got the chance?

"I'd take you myself, but I must go after Dakur before it's too late."

"What do you suspect?" Madr asked.

"I'm not sure, but we're going to find out." Zickar leaped up onto the enormous beast he'd patted, the other male mounting the third.

Only Millamay remained. She fretted, pacing as she watched the other two rush from the clearing. When she turned her sharp gaze our way, we froze, but all she did was stride over to Madr and nuzzle his hand.

"I worry she'll bite it," I whispered.

"I don't think she will." He bravely patted her head, and she purred. "See? She's friendly. This is amazing. It makes me want to seek out shayde kits myself."

I shuddered. "They killed my parents. Many of your orc females." I was having a hard time reconciling the idea of anyone raising shaydes as pets.

"These shaydes aren't killers. Dakur and the others raised them. They're clan." He lifted me up onto Milla-may's back and handed me our bags. "I'm not sure how to guide her. I hope she knows where we're going."

"And if she doesn't?" I shivered as I straddled the

lizard creature. I had a healthy respect for these beasts, but I'd reserve judgement about this one until we'd traveled with her for some time.

"We'll figure it out." His worried gaze met mine. "We have to."

CHAPTER 42
MADR

'd barely settled on Millamay's spine when she bolted from the clearing. She took a path leading away from the clan, and I suspected Zickar had somehow told her where we wanted to go.

"I thought shaydes only hunted at night," Lyneth said as she leaned back against me.

I held her in my snug against my chest and braced my legs on Millamay's sides. "She's not hunting."

She tapped my thigh nestled close to hers. "You know what I mean."

"I don't know shaydes at all, so all I can assume is that you're correct. But obviously, they're able to do what they please whenever they'd like." I patted the creature's shoulder. "I'm grateful to have her, and I'm worried about both Dakur and Brakkis. I want to look for my vox, but I worry if I don't reach the city in time, it'll be too late."

"Something could happen to your father."

"It wouldn't be too beyond belief for my cousin to . . . shall we say, hasten my father's death."

Her breath caught. "He's horrible. Do you think Brakkis is all right?"

"I hope so. I have to believe I'll find out what happened to him when we reach the city."

"You think your cousin's responsible, and not some creature or . . . maybe another clan?"

"I can't believe anyone could sneak up on Dakur, and no one would dare enter the Matis Clan and do something like that." Only a Lumen Clan member—specifically my cousin—would be so bold.

"Wouldn't Brakkis fight back if someone tried to harm him again?"

"He'd recognize my cousin and wouldn't sound an alarm."

"Even after your cousin stabbed him?'

"Jaus's message said my younger cousin, Tescall, was working with his older brother. While Brakkis might attack Riank after what happened, he'd have no reason to distrust Tescall." I growled, and while Millamay shot a glance at me over her shoulder, she kept running. How long could she travel before she'd need to rest? I'd have to trust her to make that decision as I knew nothing about shaydes except how to kill them.

She traveled longer than I would've with Brakkis, not stopping except briefly to let us drink from a nearby stream, eat quickly, and walk around in the forest for a few moments. Then she nudged my side and tossed her head toward her back.

Shaydes were smarter than I'd ever suspected. But then, they'd known how to find our females. Part of their pack had slunk into the city and attacked while we battled the rest. They'd killed so many.

As the sun began to set, Millamay's pace slowed. She came to a stop, her sides heaving.

Lyneth looked up at me. "Poor thing. She's exhausted. I can't believe I have sympathy for a shayde, that I want to do something to help her feel better."

"I feel the same." I slid off Millamay's back, helping Lyneth off as well.

Millamay immediately bounded toward the river flowing through the woods and splashed into the depths, drinking deeply.

As Lyneth and I joined her, standing on the bank, she surged up the other side and disappeared into the forest.

"Are we nearing the orc kingdom?" Lyneth asked softly. "Maybe she's leaving us, and we need to walk the rest of the way."

"Since she's covering the ground with hills and dips, weaving in various directions to avoid swampy areas or places that would bog her down, she's traveling slower than my vox. It'll take us part of a day's travel, at least, to reach the kingdom. My assumption is that she's going to hunt right now, and we'll ride again once she's eaten and rested."

Lyneth shivered. "As long as she doesn't hunt us to satisfy her belly."

The chitter of a shayde rang out ahead, and I pulled my staff from the sheath on my spine, brandishing it. But the chittering sounds moved away.

"She won't come after us," I said softly, not pointing out she wouldn't be the only shayde in the area. "She sees us as clan." I nudged my head to the water. "We need to find a place to rest until she returns. Quickly wash in the river if you want, and we'll climb a tree where we can sleep until she returns." There had been no rest while riding the shayde.

"I can't imagine sleeping in a tree." Lyneth's low laugh rang out as she removed her shoes, lifted her skirt, and stepped into the water. "Although, we slept in a tree, more or less, while we were with the Matis Clan," she said over her shoulder.

"We'll soon be inside the orc city." I didn't point out that we might actually be safer here than there. My cousin wouldn't welcome me with open arms, and I suspected I'd find him waiting along with his brother, their weapons drawn.

My belly burned to seek revenge for what they'd done to Brakkis and probably Dakur. I'd take it from Riank's hide after I'd pinned him to a wall and made him tell me what he'd done with my vox.

After we'd washed, we slipped back into the woods. When I'd found the right tree, I helped her climb, lifting her onto one branch at a time until we reached one high enough to keep ground predators from finding us, but still wide enough for me to sit with her in my lap without worrying about either of us falling.

I leaned against the broad trunk and placed my head on the top of her head. "Sleep. I'll keep an eye out for threats."

"You need to sleep too."

"I dozed while we rode Millamay."

She turned carefully to face me, wrapping her legs around me. "I think you're making that up."

"Not completely. I did rest."

"I'll sleep a bit, and then I want you to wake me so I can keep watch while you sleep."

"Of course." I wouldn't, though. I was worried about too many things.

"Don't placate me." She looked up at me solemnly. "We're partners. You're stronger, but that doesn't mean I can't do my share."

And that made me reconsider. "I want to protect you, mate."

"I want to protect *you*. I can't do it if you don't give me the chance."

"You're right," I sighed, tightening my arms around her. "Sleep. I promise I'll wake you."

In no time, she slumped against my chest, her breathing deepening. I held her and watched the world ebb and flow around us. Shaydes crept through the forest below—not Millamay—but if they knew we were nestled above, they didn't attempt to scale the tree. I hadn't heard they could climb, but I'd never heard of anyone taming shaydes before either, let alone shaydes giving orcs rides.

When I gauged she'd had enough sleep to feel somewhat rested, I rubbed Lyneth's back. "It's time, mate."

She lifted her head and blinked up at me before peering around. "It's still dark."

"About half the night has passed." A bit more, but I'd heeded her words and didn't stretch it too far. "It's your turn to watch while I sleep."

She held out her hand, but rather than give her my flail, which I wasn't sure she could use, I pulled a blade and handed that to her instead.

"Can you sleep sitting as you are?" Without waiting for me to reply, she eased off me, giving me room to shift my position.

"I can still hold you," I said.

"If you do, I'll fall asleep again, and I don't want to do that. You sleep. I'll keep my eyes wide open. I'll wake you if I see any threats."

"All right." I tipped my head back against the trunk and drifted off, but my sleep was restless. In my dreams, I kept falling off Millamay, taking Lyneth with me to the ground, where the shayde attacked us. Zickar might be confident the beast wouldn't harm us, but I'd be foolish to completely trust her, not after the shaydes had killed so many of my people.

I woke as sunlight slaked across the forest with Lyneth nudging my arm.

"We should probably return to the ground," she said, climbing onto my lap.

I kissed her, remembering being with her the night before. Would we find time for us again? Once we reached the city, we'd be busy. Life was about to crowd back into our lives.

She moaned and leaned into me, and soon, we were shifting our clothing to the side.

While I rubbed her clit, I watched the pleasure unfold on her face. Moaning, she rocked against me, riding my fingers.

"I need . . ." Her words dissolved into a whimper.

"I know what you need, love, and it's yours. I'm yours." Lifting her, I placed the head of my cock at her opening. "Take everything I have, mate. Take my heart, my soul. Take me."

I locked my eyes on Madr's as his thick cock sunk deep inside me. My gasp rang out, released because he felt so amazing. How had I spent all my life without him? Everything had been pale compared to the colors in my life now.

His spur latched onto my clit, and my eyes rolled back in my head when it started vibrating, sucking.

I was going to come undone before I'd had the chance to savor how wonderful this felt.

He helped me rise and then pressed on my hips when I sunk down, and we soon found a rhythm that had both of us groaning. The world around me faded, and all I could focus on was how perfect this moment between us was. If only everything would leave us be and let us spend the rest of our lives loving each other just like this.

When my body started spiraling, I whimpered and moved faster against him. He growled and lifted me, pushing me down to fully drive his cock inside me. It was a wonder I could last this long with his spur stimulating my clit.

Like a mudslide roaring down a mountain after a heavy rain, my orgasm rushed over me, consuming me. Madr's shout of pleasure soon followed, and we sat together like that for a moment, catching our breath. He stroked my back and whispered how much he loved me in my ear, and there wasn't anything better than that.

When I heard sounds below, I leaned over the edge of the branch, peering down through the leaves. "She's back. I think it's her. If not, a random shayde is gazing up at us and purring." When I got a good look at Millamay's face, a tremor shot through me, and I scrunched my nose. "She needs to wash the blood off her mouth. Lick it. Whatever shaydes do in situations like this."

"I doubt she bathes like us."

I backed off Madr and straightened my clothing. He only had to refasten his loincloth and somehow, that didn't seem quite fair. Maybe I'd try a loincloth and a breast binding myself one of these days.

I chuckled at the thought, and it was nice to laugh. Our situation might be dire, but I'd treasure little moments like this forever.

"What?" he asked, his lips twitching upward, though his gaze remained solemn. It appeared he'd found escape for a short time, too, but the world had crashed back into him after.

"Nothing," I said softly.

Standing, he sheathed the knife he'd loaned me at his waist and tugged me off the branch. He lifted me to eye level and gave me the sweetest kiss. I wanted to sink into it for hours.

"Ready to get going again?" he asked.

"Yes." My thighs ached from riding yesterday, and I was so tired, my eyes stung.

Madr helped me climb closer to the ground, keeping an eye on the shayde, but I was right. It was Millamay. When we were a jump above the ground still, her purr got louder.

We grinned at each other, and with me secure in his arms, he leaped down, landing solidly on the ground.

We took care of our needs and ate and drank quickly, then he boosted me back onto Millamay's spine, jumping up behind me. He'd barely tightened his legs on the beast's sides before she leaped forward, bounding through the forest.

We reached the long mountain range that stretched between the woods and the coastline by midday, and after she'd taken us through a narrow passage between two lower hills, her pace slowed.

I squinted in the sunshine at the orc city gleaming in the distance, nestled in the valley below.

"We leave Millamay here," Madr said as she came to a stop, her sides heaving.

We slipped off her back, and Madr handed me our bags before going over to stand in front of her.

He cupped her face. "Thank you, Millamay. We can never repay you."

The beast looked at me, and I read wisdom in her eyes. How could such a smart creature hunt us? Although, *she* didn't see us as food, unlike the rest of her species.

With a huff, she pivoted and trotted back the way we'd come. We watched until she'd disappeared into the forest before turning back to face the city.

I'd never seen anything like it before.

"It almost glows," I whispered, unsure if we should make much sound. Shaydes might not be hunting us during the daylight hours, but other creatures—or even orcs—might.

"We cover our wood and stone buildings with smooth metal, though that may change moving forward thanks to your sister."

"The dresalods you spoke of?"

"They climb very well but can't easily scale smooth walls. We've always lived clustered together for protection, but now that we can plant lindenmint around a home, we may no longer need the metal. We'll see as time goes on."

"My sister's favorite tea." I realized I might see her soon. She'd be so surprised when I knocked on her door. Even more, she'd be stunned that I was mated with Madr.

"We'll go to my home here in the mountains, and I'll reach out to a few trusted friends. Jaus too. I need to find out what's happening in the palace before I make some decisions."

"Will you take the crown if you have to?"

He sighed. "I don't want to, but I can't let him rule. He'd not only cause considerable damage to the kingdom, but there's also a good chance he'd kill me. You as well."

"Kill us?" I gasped out, my eyes widening. I didn't know why I was surprised. His cousin had hurt Brakkis, now maybe killed him, and we suspected he'd caused Dakur harm. He was determined to permanently keep Madr from reaching the city.

"He won't allow another potential king to live, and you're my mate. We don't know yet if you carry our orcling. He wouldn't allow a child to be born from our union, because that person would also pose a threat to his rule."

I wrapped my arms around my waist, holding back the fear threatening to burst through my skin. "You're right. We can't allow him to take the throne." When I left the fortress, I never thought I'd love the orc who claimed me. And I certainly never could've imagined he'd one day rule the orc kingdom.

"Maybe things are better," Madr said, taking my hand and urging me to walk beside him. "Perhaps Brakkis killed my cousin and is waiting at my home."

"Is that possible?"

"Unfortunately, no. If Brakkis was free, he would've found me by now."

I was worried about the gentle creature. He'd seemed so big and intimidating when I first saw him in the meadow, but he'd shown me how sweet he was, and I couldn't imagine how anyone could hurt him. "We'll find him no matter what."

He nodded.

We walked for an hour or so along a road that slowly wound over one hill after another, each bringing us closer to the outskirts of the enormous city. We started passing small, lovely homes, a few with orcs working outside. Some of them left what they were doing and approached us, embracing Madr and studying me while patting my arm. They all wished us well and told us they prayed to the fates for the king's recovery.

"He must still live, then," Madr said after the fourth person told us the same thing. "If he didn't, the country-side would buzz with the news. The elders would be meeting, and the bells would chime from the castile until they'd selected a new king."

"Do females ever rule?"

"If they're next in line, yes. My grandmother, my father's mother, was queen and her mate a consort."

I didn't know what my role might be if Madr agreed to take the crown and all that went with it. Consort, I supposed. I wasn't sure how I felt about such a thing, but I'd figure it out once we knew what would happen.

We continued to walk, Madr holding our bags, finally leaving the main road. We passed larger homes, and my belly quivered. I wasn't sure if I was excited to think I might live in such a home or scared. I was a simple person. Not royalty or from the upper echelon of human society.

Madr paused at the end of a long sloping path leading up on our left. "Jaus and Rhoslyn live farther along this road. It's close enough to walk."

I peered in that direction but didn't see anything except tall trees and swaying grass. "Do many orcs live on this road?"

"There are only a few more homes before the road ends."

At my nod, we started up a narrower track that led through sparse woods with wildflowers blooming along the sides. We rounded a bend in the path, and he paused again, watching me.

"My mother was raised here," he said, his hand sweeping out to a stately manor house sitting on a hill overlooking the enormous gleaming city in valley below.

"It's . . ." My throat tightened.

When I looked right, the ocean sparkled far in the distance. Awe washed over me, mixed with trepidation, though I couldn't define why I felt the latter. The sun shone down on the well-maintained stone exterior of Madr's home, and the well-cut stones made it appear regal. But then, he was raised to be king.

I gulped, and my breath came in short gasps.

I pinched my eyes shut for a moment and regained control, then studied his—and now my—home once more.

Well-kept gardens surrounded it, and if I didn't stress about how large it was, it gave me a cozy feel.

I could live with that.

"What do you think?" he asked, concern lifting his voice.

"It's lovely." The last of my fear slipped away. It would be all right. Madr and I would be there together. "You said it's yours now?"

"After my mother was killed by the shaydes, I inherited it. I have no other siblings other than Jaus, though, as you know, he had a different mother. My home is yours now, as well."

"It's so much bigger than anything in the village." That stabbing feeling in my belly came back, but I told myself to take this one moment at a time, to leave my fear behind. It wasn't easy, but I had to do this. Our focus now needed to be on finding Brakkis and settling things with his father and cousins, not on me and my nervousness about the changes in my life.

He took my hand and led me up a stone walkway with gardens on either side. Trees peppered the well-cut lawn, their lavender leaves rustling in the light wind.

A graceful archway encircled the upper levels of the house, and I could picture myself walking up there under the moonlight. That was comforting. The stars hadn't changed. Neither had the moon.

"It's like something from a fairytale," I said, speaking a bit of my thoughts. "You were a prince, and this is a home suited for royalty. I'm just a regular woman who struggled to survive with her sister in the village. We had almost nothing after our parents were killed. No money. We didn't even own our home. We moved into a small place and Rhoslyn worked while I went to school. I quit that before I finished because I wanted to help support us. I didn't like seeing her so tired at the end of each day or to find her quickly swiping away tears while she stared into our nearly empty cupboards. She did all she could to raise me well, but our life was stark. We had each other, thankfully, but we didn't have much else."

"I understand," he said softly, squeezing my hand.

Could he truly understand something like this? He was raised as a prince, with what appeared to be incredible wealth. "*This* home must feel small to you." As small as my voice. I didn't know why I felt so miniscule when compared to Madr. Maybe because, while we traveled, it was just him and me with no other trappings. I felt equal. Now I felt almost insignificant.

I tightened my spine and smacked myself inside. I had no reason to feel insecure about this. My upbringing had been simple but full of love, and that was what mattered most.

That equalized things because Madr loved me and, once we'd taken care of his cousins and made sure Brakkis was safe, we'd be happy in this palatial home. The orc society we'd encounter would only diminish me if I let it do so. Since I wanted to proudly stand by his side no matter what path he chose in his life, I needed to get over my insecurity right now.

I released a laugh, though it came out creaky. "I'm sure I'll get used to this. It's beautiful. I can't wait to see the inside."

His posture loosened, and he shot me a smile hinting at relief. "I can't wait to share stories of the times I'd come here with my mother. We took picnics here, escaping the city and the life we had with my father. Sometimes, we'd stay for many nights, just us and the staff."

"Staff?" I squeaked.

"Enough to keep the place clean and maintain the gardens. I enjoy doing some of that myself, but it's nice to have someone else take care of it when I'm away. There are two cooks, though no staff to serve meals. I haven't entertained here. I assume we will in the future, so I'll hire them then."

I'd have to supervise them. My belly trembled again, but I told it to stop. I'd start with simple suggestions until I felt comfortable asking for more. Surely, they'd know I was new to such a thing and would be patient with me. Madr would never hire someone who'd mock me for my simple upbringing.

We stepped up onto a low patio area spanning the front of the large building, and I paused and looked up. Each window in the two-story structure framed a different view—some overlooking the flower beds, others the valley below. Those in the back would look at the mountains.

"Would you like to go inside?" he asked.

Nodding, I gave him a smile that I hoped didn't come out nervous. It was easier to tell myself I'd feel comfortable here than act the part.

He opened one of the enormous carved wooden doors and gestured for me to enter ahead of him. Inside, I took in the open foyer with a wall along the back and archways leading to rooms on either side. A beautiful carpet patterned with flowers and leaves spread underfoot, and I almost hated to step on it.

"There's a parlor on the left," he said. "And a second parlor on the right." He pointed to the two doors on the opposite side of the entryway. "One of those doors leads to stairs and the second level, where you'll find eight bedrooms, each with its own bathroom. Our room is up there, and it's the biggest. It looks out at the mountains. The door on the other side opens to a hall with the library, a big office on the left, and two bathrooms."

I needed to use one of those soon.

"At the end of that hall, you'll find a large kitchen with a big deck outside overlooking the mountains. Another hall goes to the right where you'll find both an informal and formal dining room."

Two dining rooms. Two parlors. So many bedrooms. "How many will we entertain at once?"

"In the formal dining room? Thirty."

I gulped.

"But I rarely have anyone over but close friends."

If he became king, that would change. I doubted we'd come here more than he had with his mother while growing up. But I'd deal with that if and when I had to. For now, I'd call this pretty place my home and let my mind adjust to its splendor.

And focus on supporting my mate.

"There are no staff here right now, however," he said. "I'll notify them later today that I'd like them to start tomorrow. I pay them whether they work or not to make sure they're ready when I have need. Let me make something for us to eat. We can wash and change our clothing, then I'll reach out to Jaus and find out what's happening in the city. I don't plan to go to my father until I'm sure it's safe."

A shiver tracked through me. "How will you handle this?"

"That's what I need to discuss with Jaus. He commands the army, and he'll have good suggestions. I can't trust my cousins to welcome me into the palace, and I'm not even sure where my father is right now."

"I'll help you prepare some food."

He smiled. "Great. We can eat in the kitchen. I almost always do."

That felt . . . normal, I guessed.

As we passed a washroom in the hall, I ducked inside while he continued to the kitchen. When I finished and strode into the kitchen, I didn't find him there. Had he gone to the gardens I spied behind the house for items to prepare? He must've.

I stepped out onto the deck and peered around. Grunts and shouts from the front of the building caught my attention, and I took the hedge-lined path winding around the building toward the front. When I reached the final corner, however, I paused and crept closer to the long row of shrubs.

The shouts hadn't been repeated, but for some reason, my heart felt like I'd dipped it into a bucket of ice water.

Swallowing hard, I peeked through the hedges toward the front of the building.

Orcs in uniforms surrounded Madr.

They'd bound his arms and legs and wrapped something around his face so he couldn't do more than growl.

One of the orcs hefted him onto the back of a wagon pulled by an enormous blue-skinned creature.

"Find his mate and bring her to Riank at the palace," the tallest of them all called out. "Don't let her escape."

I slunk backward and peered around before squeezing myself through the evergreen hedge between the house and the path. There, I crouched and went motionless.

Growls and yelling were followed by the stomp of hurrying feet inside the building. They were searching for me, but I wasn't going to let them find me.

My heart drummed so loudly, I worried they'd hear. I scrunched myself tighter and held still, hoping they wouldn't think to search where I hid.

Footsteps moved along the path slowly and quietly, and I held my breath, squeezing my eyes shut. I didn't breathe again until the person had passed, moving around the corner of the building toward the front.

They continued to search, and a few times came so close, I thought they'd find me.

Eventually, most of them gave up and left, taking

Madr with them, leaving only one behind. He stalked around the building, slowly searching in a wider direction.

"They are not taking my mate," I hissed, rising from my crouch and giving my feet a chance to wake up after falling asleep. I waited until the orc male was out of view, then peered through the hedges, listening but not hearing anyone about.

With pins and needles biting my toes, I hobbled to the back of the building and cautiously went inside.

It didn't take long to search this level to find a long blade. With it in my hand, I peered out through a crack in the front door. Seeing the orc heading into the woods close to the back of the building, I scooted out the front door and raced in the opposite direction, aiming for the main road.

I didn't slow until I was hidden among the vegetation along the side of the path.

Reaching the main road, I aimed for where Madr told me Jaus and my sister lived, leaving the searching orc behind.

I strode up to the first building and knocked on the door. An older orc female answered, frowning down at me. She gaped and backed away when she spied the knife.

"Do Jaus and Rhoslyn live here?" I asked, plastering a pleasant expression on my face and tucking the blade behind me.

"What do you need them for?" she asked. "You're

human, but I haven't met you before. Were you part of the recent hunt?" She peered past me, toward the main road. "And if so, where's your mate?"

"I'm Rhoslyn's sister."

"Ah." Her face remained tight with a frown. "To answer your question, no, they don't live here. They're the next home on the left down the road."

"Thank you." Pivoting, I hurried down the path, not turning even when she called out. "Come visit again when you're not armed. I'd enjoy the company!"

I hoped I could.

At the next home, a building as palatial as Madr's, I knocked again.

Rhoslyn opened the door, her eyes widening with shock. "Lyneth? Lyneth!" She barreled into me, hugging me and sobbing. "How is it possible you're here?"

"Can you hide me while I explain?" I asked, hugging her back as tightly but feeling as if I had a target blazing on my back. "There's an orc looking for me, and he's going to hurt me."

"What?" She peered past me before taking my hand and tugging me inside.

"They took Madr, and I need help," I cried as she shut and locked the front door.

"Wait. This sounds like something Jaus needs to be a part of. Come with me." She strode down a hall and into a big office where Jaus worked at a desk.

"Lyneth?" he asked in amazement, rising. "When did you get here and . . . how?"

"Sit," Rhoslyn said softly, urging me into a chair across from Jaus. She strode across the room and lifted a tiny baby out of a bassinet where it was sleeping.

"Ah, my niece," I whispered while Rhoslyn laid the adorable orcling across her shoulder and patted her back. I tiptoed over to them, cooing at the baby's lovely face. "She's beautiful."

Rhoslyn smiled. "And I can't wait to share her with you, but you mentioned Madr and an orc trying to hurt you?"

"What's happening with my brother?" Jaus asked sternly.

I returned to the chair and sat before my legs gave way, explaining how we were mated and what happened along the way, only leaving out most of what happened with the Matis Clan. I could explain that later, or Madr and I would—once he was safe and back in my arms. I also told them about the orc hunting me at me and Madr's home. Funny how I could call it that in my heart already.

"I'll send someone to capture the orc," Jaus said, slamming his fist on his desk.

The door to the hall opened, and an orc tucked his head inside. "Yes, Commander?"

Jaus explained, and the orc's face darkened. "I'll take care of this." He left, shutting the door again.

Jaus rose and paced in the room. "We'll question him when he gets here, but it doesn't surprise me to hear that

Riank would do something underhanded like this to claim the throne."

"We need to help Madr," I said, wringing my hands on my lap.

"We'll find and free him," he snarled. "I won't allow anyone to harm my brother."

"What can we do?"

He released a chuckle that was more lethal than humorous. "Storm the palace and take him back, of course."

CHAPTER 45
MADR

T'd heard the seaside palace had dungeons deep in the ground below the castle, but when I was young, a guard caught me when I was slinking down a well-hidden back staircase, looking for them. He took me to my father, who soundly chastised me, telling me to stay away from the belowground levels of the building.

Being an orcling, I of course ignored his stern warning. But when I tried to sneak through the passage I later found in a cave inland from the castle that led to the lower levels, I found the door sealed shut. If there was another way in, I couldn't find it, though I'd explored the entire castle, knocking on walls hoping to hear a hollow sound, and trying to pry up floorboards in closets.

The dungeon had now found me.

I stood with my arms overhead, secured by wrist and

ankle manacles imbedded in the wet stone wall behind me. Water drizzled down the wall beside me, carrying with it the scent of the sea. It pooled by my feet and sunk into the dirt floor.

From what I could tell, there were four cells in the dungeon, and I was the only occupant. At least I could commend my father for that.

My older cousin, Riank, paced in front of me, pretty much frothing at the mouth, while his younger brother, Tescall, leaned against the bars and watched, his arms crossed on his chest.

"You'll never rule," Riank shouted like a proper villain.

When his guard broke into the front of my house, I rushed toward them to divert them away from Lyneth. I made it past them and out onto the front walk, where one of them leaped on top of me, bringing me to the ground. I fought, and it took four of them to subdue and bind me. When I bellowed Lyneth's name, telling her to run, they wrapped a cloth across my mouth.

They tossed me into the back of a cart and searched for Lyneth, but if they found her, they didn't put her with me. I could only hope she'd heard my call and hidden, that they hadn't taken her somewhere else.

I couldn't bear to think she could be dead, lying in the hall or on the back lawn. I'd know in my heart if they'd murdered her, right? I prayed to the fates she was still safe.

"I abdicated my place on the throne," I pointed out.

"The elders don't believe it's true," Riank said, storming up to me and spitting as he spoke.

I grimaced and leaned to the side. "Where's my father?"

"Lying in his bed, supposedly dying. I hope he is. He's lasted too long already."

"Where's Brakkis?"

His grin was anything but pretty. It cracked his face and made wrinkles appear around his eyes. "Your vox put up a good fight but my people . . . subdued him. Bound him as well. We took him somewhere and left him for the shaydes."

Bellowing, I flailed, straining against the restraints, but they held true. When I realized how happy my cousin was to see me losing control, I stilled, panting and shooting both him and Tescall a glare. "Release me, and I won't kill you."

The wisest of my cousins, Tescall shuddered.

Riank snorted and started pacing again. "You're not the one in power right now. I am."

"My father rules, not you, and if the elders are unsettled already, they're not going to hand you the throne if my father passes."

"They will if you're dead."

Tescall's frown deepened. "You didn't say anything about murdering Madr."

"Don't you see?" Riank stomped over to his brother.

"If we let him live, the army will refuse to follow me. The elders will vacillate about giving me the throne." He whirled back to me. "I'm the next in line. You gave it away."

"A big mistake if that means you'll rule. You have no idea how to lead others."

"And you do?"

"At least I've been trained."

"Why abdicate then?"

"Because Jaus is the one who should take the throne," I said.

"Your supposed brother?" he asked with a sneer.

"Just because my father refuses to acknowledge Jaus doesn't take away the fact that he's my half-brother. Everyone knows this, including the elders. No wonder they're torn. They wouldn't wish to give you a throne that belongs to Jaus."

"It belongs to me!" Riank whirled around and stomped over to the open cell door. "It's a race to see who'll die first, you or your father. Frankly, I hope you both pass at the same time. Wouldn't that be delightful?"

I didn't point out that hanging on a wall wasn't going to kill me very fast.

Tescall slunk through the opening, sending me a sympathetic look. If he had a spine, he'd overrule his brother and release me.

"Did you know I used to explore this part of the castle?" Riank asked.

"They sealed the door shut."

"Not the one leading from the shore."

I hadn't found one there. "Where?"

"In a cave. It's well hidden, but I'm savvy." He tapped his temple. "When the tide comes in, the entire cave is flooded." He pointed to grates low on the far-right wall. "They used to clean the dungeon with the force of the sea. I'll be sure to open the channels before I leave and . . . I believe it's poetic that you drown, don't you?"

"Don't do this. If you want money or power, I can give it to you." I wouldn't beg for myself. If Lyneth was able to escape, I needed to do all I could to protect her. They'd kill her in case she quickened with my orcling already.

"Money and power are the only things I can't obtain until you're dead, so there's nothing you can offer while you're alive that I need."

When I growled, he laughed and sauntered down the passage between the cells. He paused by the grates and turned a large wheel mounted in the wall, making a low rumbling sound ring out.

"Not long now, Madr," Riank said with a grin. "I wonder how long you can hold your breath before you give up and drown."

He opened a large, rusted metal door to the right of the grates, and he and Tescall left.

I struggled with the manacles, snapping my arms forward and using all my strength to try to rip them from the wall, but they didn't even creak from my efforts.

Hanging for a moment, I caught my breath, glaring at the floor.

When was high tide?

CHAPTER 46

LYNETH

"I'm coming with you," I said, grabbing a sword off Jaus's wall and hefting it. Tried to, that is. It was very heavy. But I'd find a way to use it if it gave me a chance to save my mate.

They'd caught the orc left to locate me and questioned him. He'd revealed Madr was being held in the seaside palace's dungeon, and none of Jaus's spies had been able to get inside the castle to free him. That was what we were going to do tonight.

Jaus stomped across the open living area in his and Rhoslyn's city home, stopping in front of me. He was fully dressed in armor and bristling with weapons, as were Odik and Jaus's males who'd gathered along one side of the room.

"I want to go too," Rhoslyn said, watching us both.

"You'll get in the way," Jaus told me with a scowl.

Rhoslyn shrugged, as did Eleri, who'd traveled here

with her mate, Odik, from their island home. They'd left their children under an elder, Madine's care. Odik and Eleri's oldest child, Zur, was learning Madine's tales and would one day become the keeper of their clan's past.

"I need to go," I said. "I have to make sure Madr's safe. You'd feel the same as me if it was Rhoslyn."

"Rhoslyn would never get into a position like this," Jaus snapped.

Odik nodded.

Eleri and Rhoslyn looked at each other before speaking at the same time. "We would."

"Eleri." Odik almost sounded betrayed.

"Would you remain home if I'd been taken?" she asked him, leaning against his arm.

"Of course not."

"I feel the same. You know this."

"As do I," Rhoslyn said.

"I can't take Lyneth with us," Jaus said, his voice dropping to a more reasonable tone. "Surely you can see that would be a mistake."

"You're taking all these males with you. She can stay in the back of the group. *Surely* you and your males can protect her." Rhoslyn's gaze fell on a particularly long sword hanging from the wall. "Maybe I should go too."

"No," he barked.

I huffed. "Why does my sister even like you?"

Leaning toward me, he growled. "She loves me because I am good for her."

"And good in bed," Rhoslyn said with a smirk.

"I didn't need to know this," I said, though I smiled.

Eleri grinned at my sister. "Rhoslyn and I will stay here if you take Lyneth. She needs to be there."

Rhoslyn lifted her eyebrows Jaus's way.

He took the sword from me but handed me a blade about the length of my forearm. "This is a better fit for you." He stomped his feet and grumbled; his face florid. "Stay well in the back. Do not get into trouble."

"Never," I said with a nod of thanks to my sister and Eleri. I loved it when women stuck up for each other.

"We leave immediately," Jaus said, storming to the front door with his males clustered around behind him.

"Come back to me, Lyneth," Rhoslyn said, crossing the room to give me a quick hug.

"Promise." After hugging Eleri, too, I hurried to catch up to the group. We took the stairs to the ground level and exited the building near the edge of town. We moved through the streets with only a slice of a moon shining down from above and passed through an outer gate onto the beach.

"Will we storm the palace from this side?" I asked Jaus softly.

"You must remain in the back of the group," he snapped, though quietly.

"Where I can be picked off? I shouldn't be the straggler, should I?"

He rolled his eyes. "We won't storm the castle. The palace guard will rightly protect the king even from us, and it's not fair to fight them when they're doing what they should be. Also, I don't want anyone thinking I'm hosting a coup. I know another way inside. Once we have Madr, we run and regroup. We'll talk about what we'll do after that."

"That sounds like a good—"

"We need to remain quiet."

"Ah, sorry." I pinched my lips shut to keep from talking, something I did when I was nervous.

We hurried along the beach, and I remained close behind him.

"Why not take voxes?" I asked Odik, who'd moved up to walk beside me.

Jaus sent me a frown over his shoulder.

"Those on the wall would see them, hear them," Odik whispered. "We need to remain silent."

I nodded.

We walked for a long time, our feet making almost no sound on the sand, passing rows of lindenmint plants. My sister was so smart. She was the reason the dresalods could no longer reach the city walls. I was proud of her.

The sea crashed to our right, and fortunately, the dresalods hadn't chosen tonight to attack.

Finally, Jaus lifted his arm, and we came to a stop.

He made some simple hand gestures, and one of the males crept forward, approaching a long row of boulders marching all the way down to the sea. He leaped up on top of one and scrambled across before jumping down on the other side.

We waited, saying nothing.

A cloud slithered across the moon like a dark veil, and I shivered.

Then the male jumped back up onto the boulder, hurried across and sprang down, landing softly on the sand. He jogged back to us, and he and Jaus spoke with hand gestures.

Jaus lifted his arm again, and he and most of the other males rushed toward the boulders.

I followed. They jumped up easily, but the boulders were nearly twice my size. I huffed.

Jaus paused before moving across the top. He turned back with an ever-present scowl on his face. Really. He might be good in bed but how could my sister live with his surly attitude?

He was nothing like Madr.

Madr. I'd tried hard not to think of what his cousins might be doing to him. I'd know if he was dead, wouldn't I?

Jaus must've seen my stricken expression, though how he could see much more than his hand in front of his face was beyond me. Orc night vision must be supe-rior to a human's. He stooped down and offered me a hand, pulling me up without a single grumble.

When he hugged me, it was all I could do not to cry.

He cupped my face like he had my sister's and kept his voice low. "We've found him. He's alive."

My relief sighed out of me. "Truly?"

"Truly. We're going to rescue him and return him to your arms."

"I guess I can see why my sister loves you after all."

He flashed me a tusk-filled grin. "There's no one I love more in life than her and our orcling, but I suspect you're going to be a close third."

"I suspect you'll find your way into my heart also."

"Of course." With a nod, his lopsided smile smoothed. "Now let's go rescue your mate."

CHAPTER 47

MADR

When I heard the soft whisper of footsteps, I lifted my head. If only I could rub my eyes, because I swear my lovely Lyneth was creeping down the hall toward my cell. I shook my head because I had to be dreaming.

But when I saw Jaus splashing through the knee-high water, his mace in one hand and a long blade in the other, Odik equally armed and right behind him, plus a sizeable number of my brother's best males following, I grinned. My wrists burned and bled, and my arms ached from supporting my weight, but I couldn't think of a time where I'd ever been happier—except when Lyneth told me she loved me.

Most of them stopped at the opening to my cell.

Lyneth rushed forward, flailing through the water that was coming in through the grates much too fast. She wrapped her arms around me, pressing her face against my chest. "Madr. Oh, Madr."

If only I could hold her. "Lyneth. You shouldn't be here." I peered past my brother and those with him but didn't see Riank or Tescall slinking in through the rusted door to stop what could be a rescue attempt. "Get her out of here, Jaus."

"Not without you, brother." He splashed forward and lifted his blade, bringing it down hard on one of the chains holding me against the wall. It broke apart, and he quickly worked on the other.

"There's no way you can cut through the ones securing my ankles," I said. "They're underwater."

Odik made his way to me and hefted a chisel and hammer, a grim smile on his face. He dropped to his knees and ducked his head beneath the water. Once he'd placed the chisel, he hefted the hammer and slammed it down through the water. He kept at it while the ocean continued to flood the dungeon.

Now, I wasn't worried about my cousins arriving before I was rescued. I was worried about my mate, brother, and friends drowning along with me.

Odik kept working, but by the time the water had reached my mid-thighs and Jaus had lifted Lyneth up onto his shoulder, Odik had only broken through one of my ankle restraints.

"Get her out of here," I told Jaus. I met Lyneth's gaze. "I love you. I always will. I'm so sorry we won't have more time together. But please, leave. I need to know you're safe."

Her eyes gleamed with tears, but she lifted her chin. "I'm not leaving you. If you're drowning, so am I."

"Neither of you are drowning," Jaus snarled.

While Odik kept rising for a gulp of air, then sinking into the water and beating on the chisel, Jaus handed Lyneth to one of the other males. Then he ducked down into the water beside Odik and tried to pry through the chain with the handle of his mace. He emerged, sucked in a breath, and went down again.

The water had now reached my waist.

Lyneth fretted, clinging to the other male's horns, and I could tell by her expression she wanted to plaster herself against me, hold me, as if we needed to be together during our final moment. I understood because that was how I felt about her. If our positions were reversed and all hope was gone, I'd hold her, smooth my hand across her face, and kiss her when the water engulfed us. Nothing and no one would keep me from leaving this realm at her side. Wherever we went after this life, we'd do it together.

"I love you, Lyneth," I said, not ashamed of the tears stinking my eyes. Why hadn't we been given more time? "I always will. Please take her from here, Fistard," I pleaded with the male protecting her from the flow of the water. "Get her out of here before it's too late. The passage will fill with water before it makes it way into the dungeon."

"We're not leaving," Lyneth cried, squirming to be put down.

Fistard held onto her. "I promise I'll get her out before . . ."

Before it was too late. Before I died.

"Thank you." I owed him a debt I could never repay. "Kiss me, love?"

Fistard brought her over, and she clung to my shoulders, sobbing into my neck. At least my arms were free. I could hold her, stroke her spine. Murmur how much I loved her into her ear.

"Be brave, love," I said. "Know I'm with you no matter what."

"No, Madr. It's not going to end like this. I won't let it. We'll find a way to get you out of here. I'll breathe for you. I promise."

"You can't. I want you to go before the room fills. Please." My voice broke. "How can I face this if I don't know that you'll live?" Damn, this was hard. I wanted to hold her until the bitter end, but I needed the comfort of knowing she was safe.

Only then could I find the strength to face my end with my head high and my eyes wide open.

When the water had reached my chest, I nodded to Fistard. Then I kissed my mate, my love, for the very last time.

He wrenched her away from me while she sobbed, her arms straining toward me.

I cried. I couldn't help it, and I didn't want to. I only

wished I could find the strength to stare at her stoically because her last memory of me should be me strongly facing the end.

"Get my brother and Odik out of here," I told the males anxiously waiting in the hall. "All of you. Get out while you still can."

"Madr," Lyneth cried, struggling against Fistard's hold. "Madr! No. Please, no. I can't leave you. I don't want to."

"Love you, sweet one," I cried.

As Fistard carried her through the passage leading to the sea, she shrieked with pain and sorrow.

I held her last words tight in my heart. "I love you!"

CHAPTER 48

LYNETH

I had to get back to Madr. I needed to be with him. Who cared if I died with him? At least we'd be together.

"Please let me go," I told the orc carrying me. "I can't bear it. Please. I have to be with him. He's my mate. I love him."

And that's when Madr bellowed in joy.

The orc carrying me stopped and looked back.

"Get her out of here," Madr yelled. "But we're right behind you. I'm free!"

Yes. Yes!

I slumped in the orc's arms while he splashed through the chest-deep water, aiming for the rectangular hole low on the wall that had been covered with a grate. That was how we'd entered.

"Hold your breath," he said gently. When our gazes

met, and I nodded, he ducked down and swam through the small opening where water rushed through to fill the dungeon.

Just when I thought I couldn't hold my breath any longer, and I began to believe we'd be slammed against the rocks by the surge of the tide, we shot above the water in the passage we'd followed between the boulders on the beach. A metal, cage-like barrier stretched across the opening close to the sea to keep the dresalods from accessing the passage.

The orc dragged me up onto the biggest boulder, and we remained there, crouched down while watching the exit from the passage.

Soon, more heads appeared, the orcs who'd come with Jaus.

Still no Jaus, Odik, or Madr.

I fretted, gnawing on my lower lip. I even held my breath as they must be doing inside the channel.

When I was about to jump into the sea and try to get to them, three more heads broke the surface.

Madr's gaze sought mine, and when he smiled, everything inside me stopped shaking.

In no time, we held each other, our hungry mouths meeting in a kiss that seared all the way through my bones. Pulling apart, we laughed and grinned at each other. We'd been given another chance, and I wasn't going to do anything to mess it up.

We didn't pause any longer but rushed to the lindenmint bushes and crept along between them and the wall, not stopping until we stood inside my sister and Jaus's house, still dripping water.

Rhoslyn launched herself at Jaus, and Eleri did the same with Odik. I clung to Madr, determined to never let him out of my sight.

Jaus made quick work of removing Madr's manacles and disposing of the chains from the dungeon.

"Let's dry off and change, and then we'll talk," Jaus said, leading us up the stairs to the main part of their city home. They'd left their daughter back at their mountain estate with the woman who helped Rhoslyn around the home.

In no time, the other orc males had left and the rest of us sat around the kitchen table, eating while talking about what we should do now.

"We need to get to our father as soon as possible," Madr said.

I sat on his lap. Only touching him kept me from fretting. Whenever I closed my eyes, I saw the love on his face and the knowledge in his eyes that he would die.

"I don't think it's safe to enter the palace," Jaus said.

Odik nodded. "Maybe we can get your father *out* of the palace instead."

"The guards will give their lives to protect him," Madr said. "They won't allow anyone to carry him out, not even me."

"We can't kill them in an attempt to take the king from the palace," Jaus said. "I'm not worried about my role as commander of the military. If Riank takes the throne, I'll resign. But I don't want to harm anyone who's only doing their job." He grunted; his face tight with thought. "What do you hope to achieve by reaching him, Madr?"

"He's dying. I need to be with him," Madr said.

Odik pressed his back against his chair. "He won't thank you for dying in the attempt."

"I don't trust Riank." Madr's arms tightened around me. "What if my father's not as bad off as he said? If Riank's holding him like he did me, we need to free him. I'm torn. I backed away from him, which I had to do, but he's still the father who raised me. He loves me and . . . I love him too, despite all his flaws. That's what real love is."

Jaus sighed heavily, and Rhoslyn stroked his arm, reminding me that the king had not been the same father to Jaus.

"I know a secret way into the castle," Madr said. "I found it when I was young. I used to play there until my father activated the guard when he couldn't find me. I slunk back into the main hallways and didn't tell him where I'd been, but I didn't dare play there any longer. Three of us can travel through the hidden walls. One exits into my mother's bedroom."

"Why there?" Odik asked, frowning.

Madr shrugged. "I assume a mate in the past wasn't as devoted to the king or queen as my mother."

"And what will you do when we reach your father?"

Jaus asked, rubbing the back of his neck. I could tell he had no interest in going anywhere near the palace, and frankly, I felt the same. The king didn't deserve Madr's devotion, though I understood caring for someone who disappointed you too often.

"We need to get inside before it gets light," Odik said, his gaze going to the window.

In some ways, I felt like days had passed, but it had only been hours.

"We can't risk being out on the streets with Madr unless we can keep him hidden," Odik added.

Madr rose with me in his arms. "Then let's leave now."

We armed ourselves again and left the house. Rhoslyn and Eleri came with us this time. After hearing about how close we'd all come to drowning, they refused to allow their mates to leave them again.

Keeping close to the buildings, we made our way through the streets, moving quickly toward the seaside palace. We didn't speak, and I didn't release Madr's hand. I kept picturing him pinned against that stone wall, the water rising . . .

When we reached the guarded fence encircling the palace, we quickly made our way up a side street, not pausing until we'd reached a long row of trees with branches sweeping out over the very tall fence.

"We climb," Madr said softly, hoisting me up onto a low branch, then joining me. "Don't make any noise. We can't see on the other side of the wall."

He helped me move higher with the others following. While the others waited, he and I eased out to the end of a branch sweeping above a gazebo.

With me in his arms, Madr leaped down onto the roof, landing lightly and moving out of the way so the rest could join us.

Once we were all together, he guided us through a maze of hedges, slowly approaching the side of the enormous stone palace, pausing and ducking down when guards passed. None appeared to realize we were there.

Only when we reached an open stretch did Madr stop and lift his hand. He searched the area, and we waited until he was sure the guards wouldn't see us before he tugged me across the narrow opening and through thick bushes planted in gardens close to the building. Behind them, he crept toward a knee-high wooden door nearly covered with vines. He crouched and ripped them away.

Locked.

Lifting a rock on the ground by his right foot, Madr dug in the dirt to reveal a small container holding a key. A subtle click rang out when he turned it, and the panel opened without a sound.

Greased by him in the past, I assumed.

Jaus looked startled, and I suspected this entry would be closed off permanently in the future. As commander, he couldn't leave access like this available to whoever happened to make their way close to the castle.

We took turns crawling through the opening, Madr

going first and me second. Inside, Odik tugged the panel closed and secured it on the inside.

The rest of us stood silently while our eyes adjusted to the dark.

I quivered and tugged a cobweb from my hair. Rhoslyn, Eleri, and I exchanged concerned looks, and I could tell they were as nervous about this as me, though equally determined to see this through.

"This way," Madr whispered, taking my hand again and leading me through a dark passage with stone blocks underfoot and walls made up of moss-covered granite. Dim light filtered in from tiny holes high in the outer wall that probably weren't noticeable on the outside because of shrubs and gardens.

The channel slowly sloped upward, and more holes had been added, making the going easier. After it felt like we'd made our way up one level, we came to another wooden door.

Madr placed his finger across his lips and waited until we'd all nodded to show we knew to keep quiet. He lifted a bar that kept anyone from entering from the other side and guided us into a very narrow hall with no doors and a low ceiling, shutting the door behind us.

He took a whisp lantern from where it hung near the door and blew across the creature, generating just enough light to see our immediate area.

Like the first passage, this one slowly sloped upward as it wove through what felt like the center of the castle. As our eyes adjusted, I spied small holes high in the walls that let in light from castle rooms beyond, perhaps hidden behind furniture or paintings since the light was very muted. We reached a spiral staircase and climbed that.

By the time we reached the top, I was panting, and my thighs burned.

Madr placed his finger over his lips again, though we'd all remained silent. He cracked the wooden door at the top and paused, holding his breath. Finally, he poked his head out, pulling it back inside quickly and nodding to us. All clear.

We left the stairwell and stepped into an opulent bedroom with an enormous bed, numerous ornate stuffed chairs, bureaus, and a bank of windows overlooking gardens.

The sun had poked its head above the horizon, and dust danced in the sunlight streaming in through the windows.

Madr took us to the far right side of the room and another door. His father's room must be on the other side.

This time, he didn't crack it open and peek. He swept the door open and boldly stepped inside, his hand on the hilt of the weapon sheathed at his waist. His staff rode along his spine but that wouldn't be much use in close quarters.

The rest of us followed, bursting into the room and coming to an abrupt halt.

A frail, elderly orc lay on a big bed.

He was tied and gagged.

CHAPTER 49

MADR

I rushed over to my father and sliced through the gag covering his mouth, then those tying him to the bed.

"Madr," he gasped out, reaching toward me with only his right arm. His left lay flaccid on the bed, though my cousin had still bound it. How sick was that? "Help me."

His words came out slurred, telling me he'd had a stroke or spell. He'd always been so strong and confident, but now he appeared broken. That, in turn, nearly broke me.

My heart a burning ball of sadness in my chest, I lifted him into my arms, horrified by how thin and light he was. Had Riank starved him? Who'd do something like that to our king?

"I'm getting you out of here," I snarled, wishing Riank was here so I could rip him apart. "I'll take you someplace safe. You'll recover and things . . . they'll get better." Could they? I didn't know. But he would never recover here. Perhaps in a safe place and with gentleness and care, he'd improve.

"You won't be taking him, I'm afraid." Riank snorted as he crossed the room. "Actually, I'm not afraid to say that. Why do orcs say that phrase? Anyway, he's staying here and you're . . . I'm surprised to find you here and not hanging in the dungeon submerged in water, cousin."

Numerous orcs crowded inside; their weapons lifted.

Staff and swords drawn, Jaus and Odik urged Rhoslyn and Eleri toward the door to the adjacent room. They raced forward, thrusting themselves between me holding the king and my cousin. I nudged my head toward the door, hoping Lyneth would run from here with her sister, but she shook her head, biting down hard on her lips.

The other two women hovered in the open doorway, staring at the mass of orcs in horror.

"Put him back on the bed," Riank said, striding toward me as if he wasn't worried my brother and Odik would skewer him.

"Seize him, guards," I cried. "He bound and gagged the king. He'll kill my father!"

"They won't follow your commands any longer," Riank said. "They're mine now." He tilted his head toward me. "Two of you. Take the king from my cousin and toss him onto the floor, then the rest of you grab Madr. He won't escape where I'll place him next. Perhaps the bottom of the sea, cousin? You can chat with the dresalods."

"Don't do this," Tescall said, stepping into the room behind Riank's guards. "Please, brother. It's wrong. There has to be a better way."

"The rule belongs to me." When the guards hesitated, some shooting me concerned looks, the others staring at Tescall, Riank rushed forward.

I spun away from him to protect my father, but he leaped past me and twisted, his long knife swiping out. It ripped across my arm supporting my father and sliced deep into the king's lungs.

My father gasped and looked up at me in horror. "Madr," he hissed. Foamy blood bubbled up from his throat.

"No!" Tescall raced to Riank and with a swing of his sword, he lobbed off his brother's head.

We gaped at the body as it slumped to the floor, but for only a moment.

The orcs with my cousin fled the room while Tescall strode over to me, blood still dripping off his sword. He looked down at it for a moment before it slipped from his grip, clattering where it landed. He gulped and shook his head, staring at his hands in horror. "I . . . I couldn't let him do this. It was wrong."

I nodded, unable to speak. My father was dying in my arms, and I didn't give a damn about Riank or Tescall.

"Lay the king on the bed," Tescall said. "I'll bring the healers." Pivoting, he rushed out into the hall.

I carefully lowered my father onto his bed. He clung to my arm, his gaze locked on mine, though only for a moment. Spying Jaus standing near the foot of the bed, his face stoic and his eyes filled with sorrow, he stretched out his right hand. "Son. Please. Come to me."

Jaus's spine stiffened. "What did you call me?"

Rhoslyn came over and took Jaus's hand. "He called you son." She glared at the king. "You'd better mean it."

The king grunted. "I . . . apologize to you as well . . . daughter. I . . ." He gasped and pinched his eyes closed, wincing. More foamy blood erupted from his mouth. "I'm sorry, Jaus. I . . . should've claimed you . . . long ago."

His color was leaching out of him along with his blood that pooled around him on the bed. Even if the healers stormed into the room this second, I doubted there was anything they could do to save him.

It gutted me. This male had been a stern parent, but I still had memories of how he was before my mother died. He'd loved her.

And me.

Tipping my head back, I snarled, wishing there was something I could do, that there was some way to make this right. But that time was in the past. Now, my father was dying.

Lyneth wrapped her arms around me from behind, and I leaned back in her embrace, grateful to have her with me.

The healers arrived and tried to urge us away from

the bed. We moved around to one side, leaving them to work on the king's punctured chest.

"I need . . . elders," the king gasped out. He latched onto my hand, staring up at me with so much pleading, it stunned me. "Elders. Please. Madr." His gaze sought Jaus, and he released me to latch onto my brother's hand. "Jaus. Son. Please."

I nodded to one of the healer's assistants. "Fetch the elders."

The assistant darted from the room, and it wasn't long before he returned with two of the five elders. They crept into the room behind him and came over to stand at the foot of the bed, bowing to the king.

"Jaus . . . is . . . my son," my father gasped out. "My heir."

Lyneth gasped, leaning into my side.

"What?" one of the elders cried, his gaze seeking my brother's.

"Heard me." My father took in another shuddering breath, and when he released it, more blood gushed from the wound in his chest. "Jaus. Son. Heir. I have . . . a granddaughter. Precious."

With that, my father left this world.

He left me.

And he left my stunned brother, his eldest son.

The heir to the orc throne.

CHAPTER 50

LYNETH

Three days later, we stood in the chapel of the fates built long ago on the seaside palace grounds. We'd laid the former king to rest this morning with a funeral pyre worthy of his rank, and now we'd crown a new king.

We'd found Brakkis, and he was safe. Disgruntled after being lured away from the meadow then bound and carried through the sky by other voxes, he was grateful when we found and freed him. Thankfully, the shaydes hadn't tried to kill him.

Riank had left him tied—like the king—not far from the orc city. We'd given him lots of pats and sent him to his nest to recover, telling him we'd soon visit with treats.

As for Dakur, Jaus had sent a group of his best trackers to join Zickar in his quest to find the Matis Clan caedos. We hoped they'd return soon with good news.

As we stood in the front row of the chapel, Madr squeezed my hand, and I shot him a warm smile. We'd celebrated our love over the past few days, and it was stronger than ever. No matter what life tossed our way, we'd survive it—together.

My sister stood beside Jaus on the dias at the front of the chapel, holding their daughter and the heir to her father's throne. Rhoslyn kept shooting wide-eyed looks at her mate. She'd never imagined he'd be crowned king or that she'd be the king's consort, let alone that Shirra might one day be queen. It seemed fitting, however, for a half-orc, half-human woman to take the crown—hopefully, many years from now.

Shirra was the best of us all, and I'd do all I could to help them raise her to be worthy.

My sister would do well as the king's consort. She loved our new people already, and it was clear they adored her. As we'd strode through the streets this morning, they'd chanted not just Jaus's name but Rhoslyn's.

And a few Princess Shirras.

Five elders dressed in formal robes walked slowly down the aisle, stopping when they reached Jaus.

His stunned gaze sought Madr's, and I suspected he wanted to give his brother one last chance to speak up if he wished to take the crown.

Madr dipped his head forward and the grin he sent his brother made it clear that Jaus was welcome to claim the throne.

Jaus would be an amazing king. Madr would be an

amazing king's younger brother, and that was all he'd ever wanted.

A choir chanted behind us, creating a low hum that echoed through the chapel.

The sound came to an abrupt halt.

One elder stepped forward holding an enormous, golden crown. She nodded to Jaus, and he leaned toward her. She placed the crown on his head, and when he straightened, everyone standing in the chapel cheered.

"King Jaus. King Jaus! Long live King Jaus."

"It's over, mate," Madr said, tugging me close. He leaned down and kissed the top of my head. "Finally over."

Tescall had fled the kingdom, and while Jaus sent a contingent to track him down, I suspected they wouldn't look very hard for him. As long as he never returned to the orc kingdom, he could hold onto his life. He'd played a role in saving us, and there could never be enough thanks for something like that.

Jaus took Shirra and laid her on his shoulder. He and Rhoslyn walked slowly down the aisle with the elders following. We'd join them outside soon where they'd ride through the city in a gilded carriage pulled by enormous beasts. The streets were already lined with orcs who'd cheer for their new king.

Later, there would be grand meals and celebrations that would continue for days.

"It's not actually over yet, mate," I said softly. "Your brother's reign is just beginning."

"That's true," Madr said as we joined those leaving the chapel behind the newly crowned king.

"And as for us, we've been granted a second chance."

He squeezed my hand. "What should we do with this second chance?"

"Return to your home in the mountains where we'll raise our orclings."

His brow ridge lifted. "Orclings?"

I grinned up at him and leaned into his side as we stepped out into the sunshine. The crowd cheered, a few orcs shouting my mate's name and, surprisingly, mine.

"Orclings?" Madr said again, lifting me up until we were eye level.

"We'll start with one, all right?"

"You're having our orcling?"

I nodded, grinning. "I believe so. It's not confirmed yet, but I can tell. Something inside me feels different."

"Mate," he breathed.

"Mate," I said with a laugh.

And he kissed me.

CHAPTER 51

EPILOGUE
LYNETH

Six months later, when my belly was jutting out, and I swore I waddled, we flew on Brakkis to one of the uninhabited islands close to the one where Odik and Eleri lived. We'd planned a picnic, and while we were there, we wanted to scope out the high points to see if we could build a second home.

Then we could get together with Jaus and Rhoslyn part of the year and Eleri and Odik at other times.

Brakkis landed on an open area with tall grass wavering in the light breeze. The sun shone down, and the clear sky arced above us. I couldn't imagine more perfect weather.

Or a more perfect guy to spend my day with.

Madr gently lowered me to the ground after lifting me off Brakkis. "You feel all right? No pain or anything . . . concerning?"

He was already a wreck and our orcling wasn't due for months still.

"I feel amazing. Lots of energy." Mostly. "My back only aches a little." My new normal. I rubbed it and shot him a smile.

"Sit." He peered around and spying a boulder, lifted me off my feet and carefully carried me across the open area to settle me on the top.

I laughed. "How am I supposed to get down? I'm too far up."

"Perhaps I like you up there." He flashed me a tusk-filled smile. "You can't get into trouble, my sweet one."

I scowled and put my hands on my hips. "I never get into trouble."

"You only need a little time, mate. A little time." Pivoting, he left me there with my legs dangling and strode over to Brakkis to remove our provisions that he placed on the ground. He circled over to Brakkis's head and spoke to the vox while stroking the creature's face. After giving him a kiss, Madr stepped away and Brakkis took flight.

"He promised to come back at the end of the day," Madr said, striding over to stand in front of me again.

"He didn't say that."

He gave me a lopsided grin. "Sure he did."

How could I continue to scowl when he was so cute?

"I adore you," I said instead.

"And I adore you. Would you like to stroll around and pick out a spot to build our summer place or wait until later? This home won't be anywhere near as grand as the palace, but I think you'll be happy."

"I don't need a palace or anything grand. If I want to experience that lifestyle again, I can visit Rhoslyn and Jaus. They've got at least one bedroom I can stay in while I savor being pampered by all their staff."

He frowned. "We should hire more staff. I can afford it."

His mother had not only left him the estate but oodles of money. We'd already set up a fund to help children orphaned by the shaydes like me and Rhoslyn, plus one to care for injured voxes that could no longer fly. Some orcs actually abandoned them, which horrified me when I heard about it.

"We have more than enough staff," I said. "We don't need more. I enjoy doing things for us."

"You don't need to do that, and once our orcling arrives, you'll be busy."

"*We'll* be busy." I knew he'd help. He was so kind and gentle with me, fetching me whatever my belly craved and even carrying me to the bathroom in the morning despite my protests that I could walk just fine.

He nodded.

"Other than caring for our orclings, what can I do?" I asked. "I don't like lounging around." Although, lately, I'd come to enjoy it.

"You can run the business end of our charities."

"You already do that."

"I want to start handing some of the tasks off to you."

"All right. Give me the vox charity first." I was eager to work with the voxes. One day, I wanted to travel to the Ember Clan's lands and see if a vox would bond with me.

"I will, mate." He held up his hands, and I slid off the boulder, into his arms. "I can carry you around, and you can pick out the spot for our new home."

"Madr," I warned, shaking my head. "I need the exercise. The healer said so."

"Is it bad that I love to hold you?" He kissed the top of my head and started walking up the gradual slope of a hill. After hearing about storms hitting this region, we'd selected one of the largest islands other than the main one where Odik's growing clan lived. We also wanted to be well above the sea because it tended to surge during a storm. We wouldn't be able to build on cliffs like where Odik and Eleri had their home, but we'd be elevated enough, we could sit outside and enjoy the view.

As for dresalods, we'd plant plenty of lindenmint along the shore, and Madr had a few ideas for how we could avoid them if any made it past the shrubs. Something about a smooth metal tower with a lift that would take us up to a nice room where we could wait them out. The tower would have a platform where Brakkis could land and fly us to our estate in the mountains if that was our wish.

But that was far in the future. It would take time to build our home, and our orcling would be born soon.

At the top of the hill, he paused on a flat meadow with thin woods beyond the area.

"What direction should we face?" I asked as he placed me on my feet.

"East, with the woods behind us to help provide a buffer from storms." He squeezed my hand. "What about here?"

I walked across the meadow, trying to picture what our home would look like sitting in this location. Turning, I took in the sea stretching toward the far shore where I could barely make out the gleam of the orc city. "It's pretty here. I can plant flowers and grow vegetables."

"We'll set up a desalination device like the one Eleri discovered. They're simple, and it'll give us plenty of fresh water."

"We can also collect rain. Eleri said they did that before she found the device."

What else would we need?

"I was thinking of a home with six bedrooms," he said.

"So big?" His idea of "small" was different than mine. At least I was no longer worried about managing staff and living in such a grand home.

"We need rooms for guests and for our orclings. A big bedroom for us, plus a living area, a dining room, and a decent sized kitchen." He bowed, sweeping his arm out wide. "Where I'll do the cooking."

"We'll do it together." I held out my hand.

He strode over to me and went around behind me to wrap his arms around me, tugging me back into his embrace. Leaning over, he kissed my temple. "Can you see it already?"

"Paint the picture for me."

"Stone walls with metal because we don't want to rely on the lindenmint or a tower. A broad deck on the second level where we can sit in the evening and listen to the sea." His low murmur was incredibly soothing. It was so pretty here. We were going to love coming here with our orclings. "A gazebo where we can sit and have tea."

"Screened in."

"Naturally." He chuckled. "And a big bed in our bedroom. Room enough to really stretch out."

"You don't want me sleeping on top of you any longer?" I shot him a pout.

"I believe I enjoy it when you climb on top of me, love."

"*Believe*." He was teasing me. He loved it.

"What would you say about testing out the area where we'll build our bedroom? Perhaps you can show me what you mean about lying on top of me, and I'll give you a definitive answer." He waved to an area on our left.

Ah, he wasn't speaking solely about me "lying" on him.

"I think I'm about to prove something to you, mate." I spun around, and he lifted me up for a heady kiss.

We tumbled down to the ground, and a bit later, he shouted out how much he enjoyed it when I climbed all over him.

I hope you've enjoyed Madr & Lyneth's story!

Would you like to read a bonus epilogue
from Lyneth's point of view?
It's been two months since the coronation,
and Madr's been keeping a secret from Lyneth . . .

Sign up for my newsletter
& I'll send you the bonus scene right away!

Be sure to pick up
Orc's Maiden, Zickar's story.
Zickar's determined to
track down Dakur,
but he rescues a lovely
maiden instead.
Scroll forward for Chapter 1 . . .

A new life, a new job, a new orc husband . . .
Wait, isn't he supposed to be my boss?
Find out what happens next
In Candy For My Orc Boss!

An orc science teacher is determined to
give me a lesson in chemical reactions.

Check out Orc-us Pocus!

And don't forget,
I've got a FREE BOOK just for YOU!
Sign up for my newsletter,
and I'll send you a copy of
Escorting the Alien

ORC'S MAIDEN

I'm determined to control my own life—until I meet a gruff orc who makes me dream about a future by his side.

Alwen

A year ago, one of the males in my village hurt me. When he tried to do it a second time, I took care of that problem —permanently. Then I'm selected for the annual Monster Mate Hunt where two village women must enter the forest to be claimed as an orc's bride. If an orc tries to claim me, I'll handle him just as I did the man in my village.

To my dismay, I'm captured by a band of treacherous thieves. I'm planning my escape when an enormous, snarly orc attacks the camp. He slays the thieves and announces I'm his fated mate.

I won't go down without a fight. If only I didn't swoon whenever he comes near.

Zickar

I have one purpose: to find my brother, Dakur, and bring him back to our clan. When the path leads me to Alwen, she sparks my clan pendant, proving she's mine. She fights me at every turn, and I can tell she was hurt in the past. This pretty maiden deserves to be treated gently, and I'm just the male to do it. In no time, I can't imagine a life without her.

But when someone steals her from me, I'll cross the ends of the continent to save her. Alwen's my fated mate, and I'll do anything to make her mine.

Orc's Maiden is Book 3 in the Monster Mate Hunt Series. Expect a seductive orc hero with a creative. . . (cough), size difference, a fierce, wounded woman who softens only for him, plus a fantasy world you'll want to live in. HEA guaranteed. Each book is standalone but the series is more fun if read in order.

Trigger: references to a prior assault—not shown on the page.

Monster Mate Hunt
Books in Order:
Orc's Mate
(a prequel novel –
FREE with newsletter sign-up)
Orc's Craving
Orc's Fate
Orc's Maiden
Orc's Captive
Orc's Taming

CHAPTER I
ALWEN

Tonight, my fellow villagers expected me to leave the dubious safety of our high fortress walls and enter the forest where a big, snarly orc would fling me to the ground and claim me as his bride.

I'd been "claimed" once already—though not by an orc—and I had no interest in allowing something like that to happen again.

"It's time to leave." My mother stood stoically near the door of our tidy home beside my two sisters and brother. They all watched me. As eldest, I'd helped raise them after our father died. And now as eldest, I'd take my place among those who'd been sent into the forest for the Monster Mate Hunt.

"Be strong," my mother said fiercely, her words echoed by my siblings. She bit back her sob with a knuckle pressed against her lips, but tears filled her eyes.

She knew what I'd face. She knew what happened before. She'd helped me bury the one who'd done it.

"I'll miss you so much." I hugged her, trying not to cry. I must remain strong—as always. They'd relied on that strength for years, and in this, I'd show them I could face anything. I'd leave the village fortress with my chin held high.

If I showed weakness, someone would use it against me.

I hugged each of them, sharing a bit of advice.

"Remember, when you shoot, your arm tends to pull to the right," I told my younger brother. "Then you miss."

Bredar nodded, his lower lip quivering. He was only thirteen. Much too young to have to hunt to provide for our family. But there was no one else. My sisters were even smaller than him.

"And you." I smiled as Nayleen tightened her spine. At ten, she could already create fine stitches. The best seamstress in our village had noticed and offered her an apprenticeship. Soon, she'd bring income to the family like our mother. "Keep working hard."

"I will, Alwen," she chirped, her voice still that of a child.

I turned to Creea, my nine-year-old sister. "Keep thinking about what you'd like to do with your life."

"I want to be a mom." She leaned against our mother. "But I want to be independent too." This, she'd learned from me, though I wasn't sure she completely agreed. As she grew older, she'd understand better.

It hurt that I wouldn't be here to see this, to guide them. To keep them safe.

"I'll find a way to come back to you all," I said.

They nodded, but we knew it would never happen. Only one woman sent to the hunt had returned to share her fate, and who knew if what she claimed was true? Orcs treating women gently, loving them even? I scoffed at the notion.

"I'll walk with you to the gate," my mother said. "Remain here," she told my sisters and brother.

We hugged again, and this time, we all shed tears. With them still streaming down my face, I left the only home I'd ever known for the final time. As I passed through the crowd who'd gathered along the narrow cobblestone road to pat my back, wish me well, and thank me for my sacrifice, I started to shake.

I'd done all I could to be strong after what happened a year ago. I'd proved I was a survivor.

But how would I gather up enough strength to survive this?

"The women in my family have determination," my mother whispered. "We don't let anything drag us to the ground."

"Love you, Mother," I whispered.

"We're all in this together," she said with a sharp nod, her face wracked with grief. "Remember this, daughter." Her voice faded to almost nothing. "Please, please, remember this."

"I will, Mother." Like before, I could do no less. This realization made me hold my head higher. Wipe away my tears. And stride through the rest of the town with purpose.

If those watching thought I'd comply with this, they were wrong. No need to tell them that. Once they shoved me out the front gate, *I* controlled my future, not them.

"Remember." Mother hugged me while the guards creaked open the enormous gate. "Love you. So much. Please . . ." She pinched her eyes shut as if she couldn't bear to watch me leave her forever.

After giving her a long hug, I turned toward the gates.

The fortress had been built ages ago to protect us from the vicious shaydes who hunted at night with us their prey. It was only when a treaty was formed with the orcs eleven years ago that our destinies had changed. In exchange for their protection from the shaydes, we'd agreed to send two women out into the forest each year to be claimed as orc brides.

Actually, *we* hadn't agreed. Our men had, and they weren't the ones who had to pay the price.

Lyneth, a widow from our village and the other woman chosen for the hunt this year stopped beside me, her stark gaze meeting mine.

"Shall we walk together?" Lyneth asked, and I

nodded. I had no intention of *walking*, but there was no harm in facing this part of the hunt together.

"Your bag," my mother said, rushing forward to hand one to me. The villagers prepared them for the women, and while I had no use for the skirt inside, I'd welcome the shirts and whatever food they'd tucked in at the last minute.

Lyneth and I slipped through the crack in the gate, hurrying across the long stretch of wavering grass between the village and the forest. I tried to remain stoic, to show those watching I didn't fear what would come next. But my hands trembled, the only thing that might give me away.

"Stay close with me, and you might just survive this," I said softly. I pulled the knife I kept sheathed at my side. "I have a weapon, and I'm not afraid to use it."

An chitter echoed from the forest ahead. A shayde hunted, but I was determined to be *no one's* prey tonight.

However, it was a toss-up whether we'd be killed by one of them or be forced to lie beneath a rutting orc. I shuddered at the thought and blocked out the memory of what happened.

Swallowing hard, I entered the woods ahead of Lyneth, my gaze seeking movement. I'd slash out with my blade if anything came near.

Guttural cries rang out somewhere in the distance, and my heart froze.

"Stay with me," I said. "Don't fall behind." I bolted into the woods, my pants legs swishing together much too loudly as I ran. I'd stopped wearing skirts a year ago, because they gave men easy access to my body.

I'd already mapped my escape out with a plan to run in the opposite direction of where I'd heard a large orc population lived. Maybe then, I'd be able to avoid the orcs seeking a bride. Pivoting, I started to tell Lyneth what we needed to do.

She was no longer behind me.

AFTER CIRCLING BACK but not finding Lyneth, I paused much too long to listen. Finally, I had to accept she was gone. I'd never find her. Remaining here would only see me captured as well.

Turning, I bolted down a thread of a trail.

I ran on and off for three days.

On the fourth, when I'd crouched down beside the river to refill my flask, a raggedy band of men snuck up behind me and grabbed me. They ripped my blade from my waist and one of them tossed me over his shoulder. I shrieked and flailed, but I couldn't get free.

They took me to their camp and bound my hands behind my back, securing me to a tree. While they argued about what they'd do with me, the fourth of their group, a male twice my size who appeared to be made of stone, watched.

He creaked when he strode over to stand looking down at me, and while he didn't speak, he appeared willing to do whatever the men asked him. I began to suspect stone man had very little will of his own.

My gaze was drawn to a big wooden cart parked along one side of the small field surrounded by woods. Part of the cart had been covered with bars, and someone lay unmoving on the floor of the cage. A glance around showed no beast tethered who'd pull the cart, however. Maybe the enormous stone man did it for them.

"Put her in with the orc," one of the men with long, stringy dark hair hissed, his sharp gaze shooting to the big, unmoving lump inside the cage.

"*He* won't care," another said, shifting the waistband of his pants. He wore a shirt in a bright purple color unlike anything I'd seen before. "But *I* will."

The third, a bald man, snarled. "Don't touch her. She'll be worth more to us with her maidenhead intact."

Sadly, that was taken from me a year ago, and there was no reclaiming it now.

"Stay away from her. We're going to sell her," Stringy Hair said, suggesting he was the leader.

The others nodded at his words, though stone man just stared toward the fire crackling in the stone ring.

The leader's sharp eyes scanned the open meadow. He tossed a stick of wood on the fire and sparks flew into the night sky. "Keep watch on her to make sure she doesn't get away. We'll take her with the orc to the next town, where we'll fetch a good price for them both. Then we'll get rooms at an inn and pay for what we won't be claiming from her." With that, he pivoted and walked over to a hunch of meat dangling from a tree on the opposite side of the clearing. He sliced a chunk of flesh off, speared it with a stick, and returned to roast it over the fire.

My belly snarled. The bag they ignored by the river had originally held a nice sandwich made of bread and cheese, but while I'd rationed it, it was long gone. Since then, I'd eaten berries, roots quickly dug beside the river and eaten raw, but not much of anything else. Hunting was much easier when you didn't have to run all the time and had the appropriate weapons. There'd been no time to stop to lay snares, not if I hoped to avoid both the shaydes, ashenclaws, and orcs.

"The orc doesn't look healthy enough to sell," the bald man said. Taking a stick, he went over and poked the lump lying in the back of the cart. "Hey. Wake up." He gouged the stick again. "I said . . . Damn." He shot a wide eyed gaze over his shoulder. "I think he's dead."

"He can't be," the leader said.

"If you hadn't hit him so hard in the head, he might still be alive," the bald guy snarled.

"*You* whacked him too."

"We all did, all except him." He nudged the stone man who stared down stoically but didn't shift away. "Orcs are enormous brutes. He would've killed us if we hadn't knocked him down but good."

The leader walked over to peer into the cage. "Orc skulls must not be as thick as I thought. You," he pointed to the one in the purple shirt. "Climb in there and see if he's still alive or just faking it."

"Me?" Purple Shirt said. "He'll kill me."

"I promise to bury you, then," the leader said dryly. "Do it."

At his bark, Purple Shirt sidled over to the cart.

"He'd better be alive," the leader said. "They pay a good price for orcs in Feyalon, but they pay nothing for corpses."

I'd only vaguely heard of the city perched on the edge of the desert.

It didn't take long for the guy in purple to determine the orc was dead. Snarling, the three men made the stone man dig a hole on the edge of the meadow and dump the body inside, covering him over and packing down the dirt.

"We can't stay here," the leader said. "The corpse will draw shaydes and ashenclaws."

They put out the fire and packed their things in the open part of the cart. I was tossed into the now-empty cage and when I tested the door, I found it locked. Only the green orc blood stain on the wooden floorboards kept me company.

The stone man hefted the front of the cart and started pulling it down a rough trail weaving through the woods. He kept going through the night and all the next day with seemingly no effort, only stopping at dusk when the leader shouted "halt". They'd chosen another meadow for their resting place.

"We'll sleep here tonight," the leader said. The others unpacked the cart and dumped me on the ground near a new fire, securing my hands to a tree behind me.

My belly grumbled when they started cooking meat again. The guy with the purple shirt untied one of my hands and gave me a hunk. I ripped through it, eating it fast before staring at the haunch with endless hunger.

The leader came around and stooped down behind me to retie my hands, but he paused, his head jerking up and his gaze fixed on the woods on the opposite side of the meadow.

A chitter erupted from that direction—a shayde coming too close?

I scrunched down on the ground. If they ran, I'd be pinned here as prey.

Freezing, the males stared in that direction. Even stone man looked that way.

A shayde ran into the clearing with an orc brandishing two long blades riding on its back.

Stone man bolted in the opposite direction, disappearing into the forest.

The leader strode out into the clearing, his long knife drawn, and barked out a challenge.

Foolish man. We'd established a treaty with the orcs because they were so much stronger than us.

As the orc leaped off the shayde's back, the snarling beast pounced on the leader, dragging him to the ground. The beast shredded through the leader's throat in seconds.

Gulping, I turned away, not having the belly to watch what happened next.

Purple Shirt and the bald guy fled into the woods where the stone man had disappeared.

The orc didn't give chase.

"Off," he said to the shayde, nudging the creature away from the dead leader with a tap of his knee. I expected the beast to kill the orc, but instead, it only sat on its haunches, looked up at him, and purred.

Until its gaze shot to the cage. It trotted over and sniffed. Then it tipped back its head and wailed.

A long sigh slipped from the orc, and he bowed his head, his weapons slumping at his sides. He sheathed one and clutched the sun-shaped pendant he wore on a strip of leather around his neck. "To the wind, the sea, and the mighty trees in the forest, I send your spirit. Dakur, my friend and caedos. You will be greatly missed."

"The orc was called Dakur?" I asked, struggling to rise to my feet. If I was going to die tied to a tree and from a blow from this male's blade, I'd do so while standing.

His head snapped my way. "You saw what happened?"

I shrugged. "He was dead a few days ago. They said they hit his head a bunch of times while capturing him. When they caught me and brought me to their camp, he was lying in the cage, not moving. They poked and prodded him, but he was already dead. They buried him."

"Where?" he barked.

"In a meadow a few day's travel from here. I'm not sure I could take you there, however." And why would I? The orc was buried, which was a better ending than the one I would soon face.

"Remain here," he snarled. With his weapons drawn, he leaped onto the shayde and urged it into the forest where the men had run.

"Sure," I whispered. "I'll just stay here. Think about leaving a knife, why don't you? Then I can cut myself free and run as far from here as possible."

There were no knives in sight, unfortunately, and there wasn't enough length on my rope to reach where the leader had fallen to snag his blade.

I pressed my back against the tree and waited, unsure what would happen next. The orc would've killed me already if he planned to do so, correct?

I wasn't sure what he would do when he got back, but the hollowed out feeling in my belly suggested all sorts of horrible things.

"Don't think about it," I hissed. "Think about escaping this trap as soon as you can." With a pert nod, I sat on the ground once more, staring into the fire.

Hoarse cries rang out in the distance, one after another and quickly silenced.

A short time later, the orc melted from the woods without the shayde. Chitters far in the distance suggested . . . Bile roared up into my throat, but I forced it back down. It was better not to think about what the shayde might be doing with the bodies.

The orc stooped down and wiped blood off his blades in the deep grass. He sheathed the weapons and strode over to stand in front of me, big, brawny, and much too intimidating.

When he pulled a short knife from his waistband, I flinched, though he didn't appear to notice. Instead, he stared down at the underside of his left arm.

"Dakur was my friend," he said softly. "When my parents were killed by ashenclaws, his mother raised me as if I was her own. Dakur was a year older than me, and from then on, I loved him like a brother. He was the best of our clan, the wisest and most savvy caedos we've had for many generations. No one will ever be able to replace him in my heart."

With a grunt, he slashed a line in his arm, whispering. "Dakur. May you dance among the stars forever."

My throat tightened, though I wasn't sure why. I hadn't known the dead orc, yet I felt as if I should mourn his loss too.

"I'm Zickar," he said, cleaning his knife and returning it to the sheath secured to his loincloth. Green blood trickled down his arm, but he didn't seem to care about cleaning it up.

"I'm Alwen."

"I'm not sure what I should do with—" His words choked off, and a shudder ripped through him.

As if a star had shot down from above and hit it, Zickar's pendant blazed. The light was so bright, I had to shield my eyes.

Zickar gasped. I would too if that happened to me.

He stalked closer to me and tipped my face up with gentle fingertips on my chin, tipping it this way and that to study it. His heavy gaze slide across my body with an intensity that made electricity shoot down my spine.

I was decent-sized for a woman and muscled from my years of hunting, but this male towered over me, almost twice my height and width. There didn't appear to be a scrap of fat on his muscle-bound body.

He wore nothing but a loincloth, and I couldn't stop myself from gaping at his broad shoulders, his narrow waist, and the big bulge shifting beneath the cloth bound around his waist.

He took my arm in a tight grip and stared down into my eyes with an intensity that rocked me to my core. "I, Zickar, claim you in the name of the Matis Clan."

His words were enough to shake me out of my uncomfortable perusal of his gorgeous—no, he was *ugly*—body. "You're not claiming me. I belong to myself."

He snorted. "You belong to *me*."

"Never," I vowed.

"We shall see, shall we, pretty maiden?"

Get Orc's Maiden Now

About the Author

Ava Ross is a two-time *USA Today* Bestselling author who has written numerous titles, all of them featuring sweet and steamy romance. She fell for men with unusual features when she first watched Star Wars, where alien creatures have gone mainstream. She lives in New England with her husband (who is sadly not an alien, though he is still cute in his own way), her kids, and a few assorted pets.

SERIES BY AVA

Mail-Order Brides of Crakair

Brides of Driegon

Fated Mates of the Ferlaern Warriors

Fated Mates of the Xilan Warriors

Holiday with a Cu'zod Warrior

Galaxy Games

Alien Warrior Abandoned

Beastly Alien Boss

Bride of the Fae

A Sci-Fi Holiday Tail

Monsterville, USA

Monster on Board

(co-written with Alana Khan)

Love at First Orc

Monster Mate Hunt

Single Titles

Dad Bod Dragon

Mated to the Dragon

Jasmine's Enchanted Genie

Swamp Thing (You Make My Heart Sing)

You can find her books on Amazon.

9 798869 104700